Curiosity

Ge

CH01606366

Curiosity – Geraldine Fleming

Copyright © 2022 Impspired

All rights reserved. Applications for the rights to perform, reproduce or in any other way use this content must be sent to:

impspired@gmail.com

This book is sold subject to the condition that it shall not, by way of trade or otherwise, be lent, hired out or otherwise circulated without the publisher's prior consent in any form of binding or cover other than that in which it is published and without a similar condition including this condition being imposed on the subsequent purchaser.

First Published

The Final Bet, Irish Hares and Seahorses, May 2022
Beneath Opal Skies, The Heart of the Matter, August 2022
Nola Meets the Veda, New Worlds: New Voices, August 2022

ISBN: 978-1-915819-06-2

Curiosity – Geraldine Fleming

For Oscar and Rudi
Your stories are just beginning...

'Not all those who wander are lost.'
– J.R.R. Tolkien

Curiosity – Geraldine Fleming

OTHER TITLES BY IMPSPIRED

Incandescence –
by Mehreen Ahmed

The Babel of Human Travel -
by Maggie Mackay

Pinnacles of Hope –
by Charlie Brice

The Eternals
by Ryan Quinn Flanagan

Feathers and Bones –
by John L. Stanizzi

Hometown –
by Ken Cathers

The Kingdom –
by Mary Farrell

Curiosity – Geraldine Fleming

Contents

Acknowledgements

I never dreamt I would need to pen Thank You's to a collection of my scribblings. Without the encouragement, opportunities and support of numerous individuals and groups this would not be happening. So, a heartfelt thank you to this new community so accepting of everyone, so open and patient. Within this there are some worthy of special note.

To all the members of North Coast Writers, past and present thank you for providing shelter from a changed world and nutrition for the soul. To group facilitators Mary Farrell, Robin Holmes and all my new friends who generously share their work, insights and knowledge of the craft, a special thank you. Thanks also to that wonderful organisation, U3a, helping build a bridge from the life of work to the life of retirement.

Special gratitude to Dr Kathleen McCracken and Prof Richard Bradford, Ulster University and author, Bernie McGill. Your innate selflessness and generosity took my breath away. Tribute also to Ulster University for investing all those years ago in a late starter.

To all those who read, listened, commented, questioned, proofed, edited and advised, thank you so much. Seamus McErlean, Anne Mc Glade, Sue Steging and Tom Adair for all your patience, time and support.

Endless gratitude to Steve Cawte, editor in chief of Impspired Press. He is a magician of publishing, an oracle for all things literary and a truly genuine person. Thank you for making this possible. The day I submitted some of my poetry to you was serendipitous.

And so, to my family, Malachy, my husband, who supports in endless ways and whose humour lightens my serious nature. And to Ryan, our son, who continues to educate me in the ways of the world. To my grandsons, Oscar and Rudi, your love for life is just infectious, never change.

Introduction

When Geraldine Fleming was hurled unprepared into a world of early retirement, a new life emerged. Her only routine seemed to revolve around medication times, medical appointments, coping with pain and an insatiable need for sleep.

Feeling devoid of purpose she hoped to resurrect a long abandoned interest in creative writing. Decades spent suppressing any traces of creativity in favour of professional norms seemed to present a huge barrier to pursuing this interest. Resilience though, is a wily trait and in early 2019 it lead her to the door of North Coast Writers, a newly formed creative writing group under the umbrella of the University of the Third Age, (U3a) in Northern Ireland. This group provided a welcoming, nurturing and supportive environment. It generously opened avenues into the wider writing community and innumerable opportunities to learn and hone the craft of writing. Eventually the prospect of sharing work more widely prompted the publication of poems and short stories in various anthologies and journals.

The catharsis of writing helped to shape her new world order. Drawing on life observations, experiences, feelings and ideas, continuing to expand her understanding of literature and writing skills all fed her innate curiosity. Translating impressions into words, characters, story arcs, testing various forms and genres remains tantalising.

Aptly 'Curiosity' is her first collection of short stories. There are stories that leaked from the ordinary, everyday, or strange and speculative places. Some arrived near fully formed, while others evolved from some trigger or stimulus. All are fuelled by a curious nature and the love of a challenge.

'I have no special talent. I am only passionately curious.'

-Albert Einstein

FOREWORD

By Richard Bradford, Research Professor of English, Ulster University

The short story is a literary form that seems often to deserve our pity. It is the cousin of the novel but not quite a fully respected member of the latter's esteemed family. Most eminent fiction writers have included it in their repertoire but only, one suspects, to demonstrate their versatility. How many have earned their fame by concentrating exclusively on the short form? None. Some might treat its secondary status as a reflection of public taste. In the same way that most would rather watch a gripping two-hour film than five minutes of artful cinematic impressionism so the book buyer prefers the door-stopping page-turner to the brief fictionalized snapshot of experience. But before we relegate it to the literary second division let us adopt a different perspective. In my experience as a reader of the short story – I have never attempted to write it – authors are uneasy about it because it is so difficult to master. Producing a good novel is an exceptional achievement but at least the talented writer has, with this genre, a prodigious number of possibilities and opportunities at their disposal; a broad canvas. The short story is a far more cramped space; there are fewer routes and byways for the narrative; concision – precision – is the order of the day. The form tests the resources of the writer mercilessly and I feel that Ms Fleming's natural home is the short story. Some examples:

'I Am Here' is eerie and unsettling and its success comes from the skill with which Ms Fleming carries the reader very gradually through various levels of uncertainty until, horribly, we begin to suspect why we cannot quite connect the speaking presence of the narrator with the activities of others involved in the story. Evidently they know her, but at the same time she seems at one ever-present and absent. It does not become clear until the end that she is watching them from her grave. It is a brilliant exercise in structure and timing.

'Smoke Screens' displays a similar skill regarding the subtle disclosure of truths by the slow peeling away of superficial impressions. We suspect from the beginning that there is something suspect and unreliable about the seemingly suave Louie, but until the close we remain both fascinated yet puzzled by the authentic nature of this individual. Holding the reader's attention while showing them in each passage another dimension of the principal figure is one of the most demanding skills in writing fiction and Ms Fleming is a commendable practitioner of this.

'Neuresthenia' offers us a portrait of energy-sapping screen-addiction, Involving Tyler who by the close has become all-but comatose and disembodied by his surrender to what seems to be a combination of gambling and gaming. It is very well executed and frightening; but for me, a confirmed technophobe, it provides something close to pity and relief. Once more Ms Fleming displays an impressive skill in using the various levels of her prose to draw us into the story while holding us at a distance while the full nature of the narrative and its characters move from the shadows.

'The Final Bet' is a well-executed story on the long-term effects of climate change. It will, inevitably, be attractive to those who share the convictions of the Green Movement, especially millennial readers. I admire it greatly as a piece of writing but I have a problem with using literature as a means of proselytizing ideals; but as I say, that is my problem.

'Nola Meets the Veda' strikes me as something similar to pieces by Neil Gaiman, shot through with echoes of Tolkein. It is fantastic, a little prophetic, yet the exact nature of the prophecy remains unclear. This is to its credit; black and white allegory is not enjoyable. Once more, Ms Fleming displays an enviable ability to use prose like water-colour painting, to evoke moods and states of mind in a single composition.

Something similar occurs in 'Undeserving'. Ostensibly it is an offshoot of science-fiction, but by its nature that sub-genre is limited by its self-defining features. Ms Fleming carries us into a world, our own, seemingly colonized by extra-terrestrial beings but at the same time there is a hint, just a hint, that Cathy the principal character cannot be trusted in her observations. Is it about another set of beings or a particular very ordinary human who has lost any clear notion of reality?

I have to confess that 'A Slice of Soda' is my favourite,

perhaps because I'm a fan of darkly comic realism. The techniques of slow disclosure that Ms Fleming employs in 'I Am Here' and elsewhere are at work here, but to different effect. The interchanges, the dialogue, between Shirley and Sheila (or Bella as it turns out) are brilliant. We get to know the truth about them at the same pace that Shirley becomes aware of the actual nature of her situation; an excellent stylistic achievement.

As I have stated the short story is an unforgiving genre. Treat it, lazily, as a brief novel then the flaws will become conspicuous: the reader is more aware of what might have been than what is. Ms Fleming, however, tackles its intrinsic complexities courageously and successfully. She uses it not simply to tell tales but rather to show us how much we rely upon language for a sense of identity and self-possession. Typically, her characters and speakers bring us into their troubled worlds so that we find ourselves sharing their troubles but not simply as problems described; we become, like them, prisoners of a state of mind in which words at once tell us something yet withdraw that promise of meaning and certainty. It is an extraordinary collection.

Curiosity – Geraldine Fleming

A Slice of Soda

Shirley relaxed her shoulders just enough to remove her kid gloves and stow them in the crocodile handbag braced in the crook of her arm. Curling her fingers around the shiny brass knocker she gave two brisk taps on the over-painted door. Fibres from a recent encounter with Brasso gritted her fingers, clinging to her red nail polish. She almost tutted as she snapped the clasp on her bag, the clatter returned her to the morning's task.

So far not one furtive net curtain had noted her arrival. She had parked on the main road and walked through the tight hodgepodge of streets to the address, 79 Warnock Street. A cold wind whipped along the narrow street catching barely a single fragment of dust to reward its effort. Shuddering she rapped the knocker again, harder.

That morning she hadn't eaten breakfast. Instead, she carefully chose her outfit. A fitted maroon two-piece suit teamed with a camel swing back coat. She had taken special care with her make-up too, the expensive pressed powder hid sunken dark hollows under her hazel eyes. Covered her exhaustion.

Still, no one answered the door. She could feel her plan unravelling much like her courage.

Just one more time, then if there's no answer- if there's no answer I'll just have to come back later.

Leaning forward she made a fist and hammered the door three times.

Well, if there's someone home, they'll have heard that- whole bloody street probably did.

Shirley held her breath, listening for the sound of a bolt drawing back or a neighbour asking what she wanted. Nothing happened. Just as she was about to leave, she heard the slow scrape of a lock turning.

As the door opened, she rehearsed her speech. One delivered so many times before. At so many houses and flats on so many streets, to so many women.

How many times now... exactly? She asked herself.

Why pretend you can't remember. This brings it into double figures.

She swallowed the rising bile, breathed hard through her mouth and prepared to greet the occupant. A small plump, red cheeked woman stood in the doorway. She wore a nylon apron over her floral blouse and black skirt. With grey hair still in curlers and bound in a pink hair net she resembled a little Russian doll. Shirley stood open mouthed; she could not speak a word.

'Yes dear, can I help you? Have you been knocking long?'

'Sorry to disturb you, I'm looking for Sheila.'

'Yes dear.' Looking down she wiped her hands on the apron.

'Now if it's insurance, I don't want any. And I'm not one for buying anything on tick if that's what you're about.'

For the first time Shirley's lines didn't fit this scenario.

'No, nothing like that Sheila, may I call you Sheila?

At that moment another cutting blast of wind raged the length of the street and Shirley shivered.

'Look it's cold, you're freezing there. You're nearly blue. Come in ... as long as you're not selling anything?'

'No, I promise I'm not selling anything.'

***

Sheila opened the door wider. Looking over her shoulder she led the way along the narrow hall. The house seemed familiar. Shirley drifted toward memories she felt belonged to someone else. She could feel the swing of girlish white-socked legs, tap impatiently against a chair runner waiting for soda bread to be delivered from her grandmother's range.

Sheila turned off the radio.

'Sorry I like to get the morning news. The world these days ... well what can you say.'

Sheila shook her head of curlers as if to dislodge an annoying thought. The table had rings of flour and sticky baking debris.

'It's warmer in the kitchen. I'm just baking soda bread. Have a seat and I'll get us a cuppa. Get you warmed up. I keep meaning to get one of those new ding dong bells, I don't think there is a lot of point now.'

She busied herself with tea making. Giving the younger woman time to settle. The smell of fresh bread lit up the kitchen. Resurrecting long lost hopes and dreams.

'You're baking.' Finally, she found something to say.

'Yes, usually I bake on a Tuesday but I've a hospital appointment tomorrow so it's all a bit of a rush. But I've it finished now.'

Setting two china cups and a steaming teapot on the table Sheila sat down with Shirley, one at either end of the now immaculate table.

For the first time they openly studied each other,

Grand Masters deciding on their next moves. Shirley didn't think she could trust herself to talk without crying. The unexpected situation, the force of memories disarmed her usual staid presence. She lifted the tea and began to sip. It was strong and sweet, she hadn't noticed the milk and sugar going in but it was like nectar to her. The reviver began to thread its way toward a deep coldness. Sheila held the silence a little longer.

'How are you now? she ventured. 'Thawing out I hope. This road is the coldest place on earth. I wouldn't be surprised if an iceberg floated past my door.'

Catching Shirley's eye, she held it for just one moment longer than necessary.

'Well now, I think you were about to tell me your name. Oh, would you like a slice? I think we could risk a round with butter and jam.' Sheila nodded in the direction of two bumps of loaves draped with linen towels.

'Yes please, that sounds lovely. I'm Shirley... Shirley Longshaw.'

She stretched out her hand just as Sheila set the fresh bread slathered in butter and jam on the table.

'Pleased to meet you, Shirley.'

Their hands clasped, as different from one another as they could be. One manicured, soft and delicate, the other strengthened by hard work and gnarled by years. A gentle vitality flowed from one to the other.

'Eat up Shirley and then you can tell me what it's all about.'

'I came here to talk to a woman called Sheila, a woman I believe my husband is seeing. I came to ask her to stop the affair.'

She had voiced her petition yet she was sure Sheila was not the other woman. The others were always younger, prettier, looking for something, true love, a helping hand in their career, or just a good time, dancing, holidays, gifts. She had an approach for each type once she knew their motivation. If a heavy dose of guilt or shame didn't work she found the money in the white envelope in her bag was a winner- *break it off now!*

In the kitchen oasis the ticking clock held the heartbeat of their existence. Sheila watched the younger woman's conflicts tumble, like shafts on a lock against the wrong key.

'You know I am not the other woman. I've known other women but never been one. This is not the first time you have intervened, is it?'

They had moved to sit in fireside chairs either side of the range. Both nursed their teacups. Shirley traced the tiny flower pattern around the china cup, watching the darkness of her shadow-finger. There was only tenderness in the other's face. No reproach, or disgust or shame. With shock she realised those devils just lived inside of her. Tormenting her.

'Yes, I know that. I was the other woman once. I'm... I'm paying for past pain I caused. I met him when I was eighteen, he came to work for my father. He was married, I knew that. I'm thirty-two tomorrow. This is the tenth time I have come to speak to the other woman.'

She wanted to hang her head in disgrace but Sheila's presence seemed to hold her firm in the orbit of the room.

'Ten you say... What a busy man Mr Longshaw is. Do

you think he'll ever stop?'

The question hung like a banner strung across the hearth. She had never considered this before. Always the effort was locate and defuse, like dealing with an unexploded bomb.

'Busy... yes. Practically one a year... that I know about. Do... do you think he will stop? He's bound to just settle soon... isn't he?'

Despite the plea in her voice Sheila could not lie.

'It'd be wrong of me to tell you just what you want to hear. 'Specially when you already know the truth, in your heart. You've always known really.'

Shirley's emotions flooded over in the starkness of a home truth. She wept. She wept long and hard for lost years, for twisted devotion and vain hope that things would change, that he would change. She wept for lost opportunities and the guilt she carried. She cried for all the maybes', maybe if they had children, maybe if he hadn't been successful, maybe if they lived in a different town, if she was prettier, funnier, sexier, taller, smaller. As the list gathered speed the absurdity of it all struck her. All through the outpouring the steady strong arm rested around her shoulder and smuggled in hankies through the gaps in wails and blubbers. Sheila never muttered *don't cry* or tried to stem the flow, she understood it had to be excised. The wound was laid bare and the salt, now stinging would later cleanse. Eventually, a steadiness came over Shirley, part exhaustion, mostly relief. Within the haven of the small room barriers dissolved. Fortified by memories of long-ago slices shared, and an encounter with a stranger a new kind of understanding took seed.

'Sorry … I have never been like this. I really ought to be embarrassed but oddly I'm not.'

'Nothing to be apologising for. I think you need another cuppa, I know I certainly do.'

Again, she busied with the tea making. This time she placed two large mugs on the edge of the range.

'If I had whisky I would put a tot in but I'm not a drinker so extra sugar will have to do the job.' She lifted her mug as if to toast the event.

A sudden thought occurred to Shirley.

'Is your name really Sheila?'

'No... well you have me there. Sheila lives 79 Warnock Street, this is 79 Warnock Road. She is two streets over and one up.'

'I don't understand. Why'd you say yes when I asked at the door?'

'Truth be told, Shirley only desperate wives look for Sheila. She likes married men. Likes to humiliate the wives who come to her door. I just thought I could save you that. I'm sorry I just did it on the spur. I'm Bella, that's my name... Bella Hope.

***

In the silence, broken only by the coals in the fire rearranging themselves Bella flicked breadcrumbs off her apron. Allowing a long-held secret to surface she spoke in a whisper.

'She makes a game of it you know. Who she can entrap, who will come to plead for their husband back. She was nineteen and just testing her power over men.

The Catherine Wheel burns bright and fast. I just let it run its course. I forgave him.'

'God, Bella.'

Shirley leaned over and squeezed her hand. Bella mopped tears with the corner of her apron and smiled. Shirley understood this was not pain but sadness. They sat at ease listening to the pings of the cooling oven and the ticking clock, each deep in thought. Though not dissimilar thoughts.

'I think he is like that too you know. Leaving trails for me to follow. It's a game to him too. But this is not a game for me, not any longer. I'm not a piece on a chess board.'

***

Long past lunchtime the door to 79 Warnock Road opened. Shirley's face, free of the remains of her tormented make-up, shone in winter sun.

'I'll call over at nine in the morning. We will go to the hospital together... And please Bella... answer the door.'

The Final Bet

Jada sighed hauling her near empty tanks through the final air lock into the small grey chamber. Dim lights cast their slow shapeless shadows across the arced walls. Weakened by exertion and in dread of the next stage, four divers hook their tanks to the reload station and slumped into the medical nooks. The alcoves woke at first touch. Intelligent devices slid connections into their neck ports. It was as always a matter of wait and see.

No one spoke.

They all struggled to breathe. Their bodies engaged in the battle between gases and pressures, between demand and supply. From her nook Jada studied the other Foragers. They were the picture of exhaustion. Asher, grey with deprivation, bit his lip to distract from the confusion swarming in his head and the rip of oxygen starved blood pleading with his lungs. His eyes were closed, head nodding to synchronise his breathing. Cortic pressing hard into the nook stretched her legs into the middle of the chamber. She focused on a random spot on the wall as she massaged and slapped her ribs, her own technique to rouse her lungs. Mercer's pressure suit was rolled to his waist. His torso, tinged blue-green in the strange light, was just starting to pink as his respiratory system began to feed his circulatory system. Fists clenched he took great gulps of air like a feeding basker.

Still, no one spoke, each caught in their own battle for life. All Foragers had coping tactics, there was a rumour one scavenger did handstands, though Jada doubted that.

The 'struggle' was routine, natural. Many compared it to being born again and again. Jada knew the drill. With training, experience and a few genetic edits their lungs would regain control. They would walk out together, meet the director to log the salvage and then sleep. But before that came the pain.

Asher cleared his throat, 'How long left?'

Jada sat beside the dials and prepared to call off the figures.

'OK, scores say we risked it out there. We need a longer acclimate this time. Mercer and Cortic, Mother wants you to sleep so expect that drug delivery… now. We will be repaired and released in 2 more hours. Nothing too devastating this time you will all be glad to hear.'

Before the breakdown in their supply line from the surface, Foragers floated out a few times a week to gather data and samples for the various studies located on the Perdix Suboceanic Base. Now the Foragers were out everyday, on rotation three groups of four scouring the sunken towns and cities for anything that would be useful. Sometimes they had a list, other times it was opportunistic. With the disruption above, their scouting was now critical to the survival of the small underwater community.

She tapped to confirm the medications.

As Mercer and Cortic drifted off she activated the view screens.

'It's better than listening to our breathing echo round this damned room.' She avoided meeting Asher's puzzled gaze.

She wished Mother, the medical module, had

prescribed her sleep too. Instead, here she sat as nanites recalibrated her cell by cell.

'What d'you think the header will be today?' Asher tried to smile but the effort was premature, his face configured a smirk instead.

Personal grid updates had faltered and then ceased months ago, the underwater community now relied on older tech. The familiar news cast filled the screen. Jada pretended to consider the question as something serious. Her dark curls bouncing from shoulder to shoulder.

'Well now, let's see. Could it be the failure of the wheat crops in the Sahara due to water contamination? Or finally the breakthrough in predicting the movement in the tectonic plates? What about the discovery of new sources of renewable protein? Or the communications impact of the latest sun flares? Or even the number of launches this month to Moon and Mars colonies complete with population figures? No, I give up what do you think?'

Asher's face managed to move the right combination of muscles and he sat opposite her grinning.

'I don't think I have ever heard you say so much in all the time we have been together. Perhaps it's the meds.'

'Yes sure it could be that or it could be that we're all trapped in our own worst nightmare... Sorry... I'm just on edge.' She closed her eyes and slumped back into the nook seeking some comfort in its familiarity.

Asher shrugged. 'Understandable. You definitely didn't sign up for this. Not your fault your father's the director.'

Jada blinked away the taste of sea tears.

'He says 'scavenging is a privilege'. Not one I'd have chosen though, not like this.'

'It is a privilege Jada, you understand why he brought you with him when he took this assignment, don't you?'

'He took me away from everything and everyone I know to do what? Live here with a bunch of nerds and old people.... Anyway, you don't even like him... why pretend you do?'

The words tumbling from the news report cut across the tension. Silence fell between them as the unimaginable entered reality.

' Attention, attention. This is a looped emergency recording. Evacuations are proceeding according to the 2222 emergency plan agreed by the confederacy of world powers. In the last two weeks you received your personal safety plan. Now is the time to follow those instructions.

With the escalation of land wars on the three remaining above sea level land masses we have been instructed to evacuate this station. In recent days the regulatory forces have been overpowered, overrun by the combined opposition forces. How humanity survives - if we survive- is now on the throw of the dice. As you all know the plan spreads our bets. In space, under the seas and on the small lands that survive humanity will adapt and strive to survive until the waters subside.

'Future reports from this outlet will be delivered from Moon colony ten. Take action now, do not delay. Best chances to everyone. Attention, attention....'

Neither of them spoke.

Beneath Opal Skies

'That's the best bad idea I've heard so far.' Leo clapped his heavy-duty gloves signalling the end of the meeting.

'After all, we can't disappoint our families, can we? Never have before... it's not starting now.'

Glenn and Willis nodded conceding the discussion. With solemn shrugs, they strode toward the shaft's exit ladder. Tunnel spoil crackled under boot and the dry dust of recently jackhammered sandstone clung to the dense air. Their retreat was based on years of 'Leo experience'. He would want them to leave the mine, give him time to think, time to formulate. Since his collapse the future had taken a pale grey pallor, much like Leo himself.

Their hard hats broke ground level. Body sore and shading their eyes from the bald sun they set off over a pockmarked wasteland. Two giants miniaturised in the vast belly of the landscape. Sidestepping mullock heaps en route to their trailer. Usually, they would have staged a stronger resistance. Many times, anger blazed between the three brothers, hot and personal. Leo led by example, that was his motto. In the Tavern at each end of season celebration you could hear the boom of his voice as he took some newbie asking advice to task.

'Never, ever, ask a man or a woman to do something you wouldn't do yourself, full stop.'

Now though, everything was changing. Dynamics in flux, a yawning chasm as the threesome silently negotiated new lines, new dissections and new tolerances.

Alone, Leo turned to face the load-bearing wall, the focus of their discussion. Halogen lights cast his fading shadow as he paced the hewn verge. Camouflaged in apricot dust he hunkered on the floor, pushing down his newly-prescribed mask he ignored ragged breaths as he ran calculations through his head. He picked a spot on the roughcast wall and stared with laser precision. Dazzling green eyes flickered and his square jaw clicked as he sketched imaginary lines and dropped in audacious figures intent on achieving the goal. A long absent smile interrupted the lines on his face, craggy hands smeared unexpected tears.

He had promised himself no tears sitting in that hospital bed. The cardiac consultant stepped back between the pink cubicle curtains, leaving Leo adrift in his alternate world. He missed filler words completely but the significant parts, those life chilling phrases clung to the fog-swirl in his brain. *It's serious... heart disease...no exertion... need to change your work... talk to your family.* He marvelled so few words could change his life, his future, everything.

A brilliant engineer, Leo had no interest in the tens of millions of years taken to form opals. He did not dream like a geologist of water percolating silica through strata of sandstone, settling in the cracks to eventually form precious gemstones. Instead, he dreamt in marvellous technicolour, opals iridescent in their splendour freed from their earthly tombs. Diffracting flashes of colour sang to his heart. Above all else though, was his heart's desire, the most beautiful, most valuable opal, the enigmatic black opal.

Leo read indicators, the shorthand of stone told him where to aim the jack and usually he was right. He always said hitting a good seam was fifty percent calculation, twenty-five percent intuition and the last twenty-five just sheer bloody determination.

He was an opal hunter, that was what he knew. It coursed through every cell, coded every synapse, it was his last thought at night and first in the morning.

Each season the quality of the finds sustained their families and financed the next season's hunt. They all enjoyed a good living, some years better than others. This season's finds for the trio had been scant, barely covering their overheads. Their search for the elusive opal bearing seams remained just that, elusive. Leo's absence weighed heavy on his brothers and their families. Worry lodged in everyone's heart, though with respect little was said once Leo outlined his plan. No one wanted to think about the future, remaining wide-eyed in a strange world. Admittedly the level of risk in this dig was one Leo would not have considered acceptable, not in the past. Yet he had twisted and turned in his usual emphatic manner until he got his way. In truth though, they were short on options.

In the trailer they kicked back after their first lager and a spruce-up, waiting on Leo. Glenn strummed his tuneless guitar, plucking chords like random thoughts. Willis leaned easy against the galley unit slicing and dicing vegetables. Relaxed now, they reran the plan, teasing it back and forth until they felt they had their moment unclouded by Leo's conviction.

Over the years they had outvoted him only to end up squirming in regret and lighter in their bank balance.

'You remember the time you broke your leg in that

landslide? Jesus, I thought Leo was going to kill us himself.'

Glenn struck a particularly discordant note as a memory pain shot through his leg.

'Well, you can understand, he did say *don't dig there.* He was specific. Lucky it wasn't worse.'

'True. That leg still gives you bother.'

'You got us a shed load of bother when you used that new appraiser. Instead of Jake... all 'cause you thought you could get a better deal from a Sheila. She ripped us off ...big time... You always were a fool for a pretty face.'

Willis tossed the rolled-up towel at his brother only to receive a slapstick return.

"Thanks... I'd finally managed to forget that and you bring it up.'

Glenn rested his guitar on the floor, Willis straightened the towel, an air of seriousness returned to the trailer.

'What d'you think he's doing down there?

'Just thinking, planning this stunt. Praying it works. Trying to shoulder it all himself.'

I guess, he'll come in soon to eat... Jeez I just thought about that time with the jack compressor. He was in the ballroom giving it full throttle when that bloody thing just spluttered to a dead-stop. And then ... and then you tried to bluff him we'd serviced it, when we hadn't. God...now that was unbelievable. We let him go to Darcy's Fitters before we admitted we hadn't taken the damned thing in.'

'Yeah ... and when all the yelling was done, he said it was the lie annoyed him most.'

'Mm-mm that one I never forgot.'

***

Leo was established as the voice of reason, he worked the margins well for the brothers over the years, steering close to the cliff edge, always the right side of gravity. True to his prediction his younger brothers never raised one doubt about the wisdom of removing the supporting wall.

The expense had all but cleared out their stake and savings. New pillars and props, great felled trees, wedged tight with chunks and then slimmer cuts braced the roof. Leo supervised the work and within the week they were ready. The consequence was unspoken, succeed or fail after this everything would change.

'Right then.' Willis said lifting the jack. 'Where do you want to start?'

Leo swept his torch beam over the rock surface, he knew every contour. He patted the bare rock like a friendly old dog.

'Here Willis, gentle just here... This is the sweet spot.'

They gathered in the ballroom, seventeen metres below ground. Taking out the bearing wall required the suspension of reason, old school thinking and faith in Leo. The jack hammer punched rock. Glenn began to lift and clear the spoil into the vacuum while Leo unaccustomed to this enforced inactivity stood against the wall. With each series of strikes they halted, checking the props and Leo stepped forward to rub shards off the rock face. The demolition continued in their efficient silence.

Glenn saw it first. A dark glint in the unnatural light. Howling he yanked Willis back from the wall. The jack pounded empty space in the fraction it took to release the throttle. Forgetting the warning about overexerting himself, Leo dragged the lights closer, shadows stretching the darkness left behind. He tilted one blinkered stem onto the jacked spot. There it was, unmistakable, the seam revealed itself to them. Every element in the universe spun around that exact moment, pinpointing that exact scene. This was their discovery, their God Particle, black opal.

Gently, with precision, they gouged away the ancient crust of rock. All eyes locked on the wall, straining, breath held, hearts tripping with excitement... They worked and the seam expanded and expanded. Shielded from the outside, existing only in their own hollowed out world the trio pitched between awe and elation. Over two days they uncovered a record-breaking haul, enough black opal to stake many years hunting, enough to cushion financial worries.

On the third day with the seam denuded, the trio stood above ground. In the midst of a scraggy pale salmon landscape and blue opal sky the brothers gathered around the sagging appraiser's table. Jake, struggling to maintain his professional demeanour, had confirmed everything they expected and so much more. Faces streaked with tears, they whooped and hugged. Brothers united in birth and bonds. Feeling the narrowness of Leo's once sturdy frame, reminded the brothers of the seismic shift in all their lives.

Jake offered his hand in congratulations. Years of finds

and haggling and respect spilled over as he was pulled into the brothers' bouncing embrace. With the haul safely locked up in Jake's ancient safe and the money transferred to their business account the only thing left was a 'deal closed' drink.

'Shall we retire to the Tavern? A drink and a bite to eat?'

Jake only had to ask once. They walked the dusty street like gunslingers, no spurs, no guns but a swagger in their step.

'Well, boys what do you think of big bro's new venture? You think he can help those newbies sort this game?

'I think *Leo Anderson Consultant Engineer* has a ring to it. They are getting a lifetime of experience from the best... the very best.'

Glenn nudged Leo's elbow.

'Show your business cards... '

Leo set a stack of pristine cream cards in the centre of the table. Each lifted one in turn, like cutting a deck for winner takes all.

'Mm-mm classy... great reference to the biggest black opal find... to date... Holds out hope. Good selling point.'

Willis held the card moving it back and forth appraising its virtue and value.

'Look at all those letters after your name. Guess all that study wasn't wasted.'

Glenn whistled a low note of appreciation.

'Time you both tried a bit of study yourselves, use the brains God gave you. You need more than one string on a manky guitar in this life. Never know... I could be putting work your way. Remember... I'm still a partner and not a bloody silent one either.'

Leo stood proud, a different future crystallising before his eyes. He was beginning to appreciate the geologists' long perspective. When conditions align opals form, sometimes they differ in colour and grade, all are beautiful, all are unique. He raised his glass to the gathering.

' Well, isn't life strange... Seems to me there is not just one path for any of us. I sure got butt-kicked into a different world... But you know what? Sometimes forced change is what you need...what we all need. So, it's cheers to change.'

Glasses raised, the gathering drank to their new world, full of potential.

'What I want to know is how will you share an office with Jake? He isn't going to pander the way we do. You won't come home to a cooked dinner every evening.'

Willis eyes danced as he enticed Leo to rise to the bait.

'Never you mind with that. We will be fine. Makes sense this way, share costs, share customers. I'll do family rates, by the way, when you need me.'

Leo winked at his brothers and further afield, a general wink to the universe of infinite change.

Undeserving

The penetrating alarm failed to drag her from sleep, from the void of her late-night medication cocktail. Her breathing was shallow, eyelids shielding her from another nightmare. Consciousness struggled, bobbing in the opioid sea she fed herself nightly. Then she heard him, beyond her alarm, beyond the miasma.

'Mum, Mum, time for brekkie, time to get up.'

The light chimes of her son's voice provided an antidote of adrenaline. Her hammering heart and rushing blood forced her fogbound mind to form the thought, to trigger the movement.

Cathy bolted up. She dumped the alarm and arranged herself like a new-strung puppet ready to take her first step.

'Coming Ettie, my sweet-pea. What do you fancy for breakfast?'

She pulled her bedraggled brown hair into a knot as she made her way to the kitchen, oblivious to the debris of her unattended home. Ettie was not in his usual seat at the table. He was not swinging his tanned legs, stretched by a recent growth spurt, singing to himself.

'Oh Ettie, so its hide and seek this morning. OK, ready or not.'

The unfamiliar crease of a smile replaced her ingrained grimace.

'Bet you're in the garden. I'm coming to find you.'

Echoes of her playful lilt broke the silence as she leaned over the kitchen sink to check the garden. Not for the first time, the stinking dishes rearranged themselves. From the corner of her eye, she fancied she caught Ettie's heel nip into his bedroom.

She beelined there next. Empty. The spotless, cosy room, was estranged from the neglected house. A neat bed, an abundance of shelved toys and knick-knacks betrayed its status. Reality crashed in, driving a distraught Cathy into the bathroom.

She buckled to the floor at the sight of the Kl'qui drug caddy perched like a homing beacon on the side of the sink. Opened only by her fingerprint, it released to her touch. Her breath was ragged and the prism of tears diffused the jewel-coloured pills. Something to help no matter how you felt, or didn't want to feel. Clicking out two citrine pills she swallowed them dry and waited for the initial wash of calm. A crutch to cope with melancholia, a treasure chest of numbness and if you chose, finality. The Kl'qui were not unsympathetic. The golden triquetral insignia taunted her, forcing her to remember. She tried focusing on the lines of the ceramic floor, she knew they scored straight across in squares, but not yet. Pressing herself against the tiles she swiped waves of despair from mid-air replays.

Reliving gatherings of families and friends, bubbling with excitement, eager to receive the wisdom of an advanced culture, humanity's benefactors. Six months after first contact the Kl'qui visitors spoke to the world, global media was awash with speculation. How would the visitors introduce them to the other races, how would they share their technology and enable advancement. So many possibilities, so many futures, galaxies to explore. The visitor's technology enriched the human race's understanding of the universe, reinventing their understanding of existence, of sentience. Even those inclined towards conspiracies were hopeful in their speculations.

The Kl'qui assessment of the planet changed everything. The message was short and ice-cold, humans were undeserving of their world and thereby undeserving of the children of Earth. She shivered and shrivelled away from the memory, optimism and hope turned to shock and despair. That was the moment, in her opinion, the world plunged into dark chaos. Earth's representatives tried to engage again and again, tried to negotiate the children's' return, everyone held their breath, hoping and praying, The Kl'qui's motives were inscrutable. Global impotence spawned world-wide melancholia. So many friends gave up hope within the first few months. She had attended funerals almost daily, the grief of their loss robbing them of life.

Each day began the same for Cathy. First the density of denial, then an assisted struggle to function in the new reality. She managed to stand up. After the medication she was always gripped by a fierce thirst, she drank from the faucet. Barely recognising her image in the mirror, she moved her lips, thin and blue. Her words unsynchronised, like some badly dubbed actor. She ran her trembling hands over her face, digging palms into her eyes.

'I don't know you. What the hell happened you?'

Hollow-eyes, waxen face, hunched shoulders and aged beyond her forty years she began her ritual of recovery and reinstatement, raising cupped hands of water to her face. She only wished she could say it felt good. Nothing had felt right since she lost Ettie. All the Earth's children were gone, four years now and no children had been born. Fetuses disappeared from wombs and no one could conceive. One day the children were there the next everyone under sixteen was gone. Ettie would be ten.

Within thirty minutes she had showered and finished her first coffee of the day. She perched the fusty cup back on the crockery mountain. Allowing herself to blind-eye the family photo, she pushed on with her routine.

Her husband, Finn had left. He accepted the Kl'qui's resettlement offer and left for some new world. She had watched the armada leave orbit two years ago. They left their home planet on a trail of lost dreams and fractured futures. There had been no contact from the leavers, the armada had gone silent. Cathy knew she would never see Finn again. She chose to remain at home, hoping the children would be returned. The photo framed the world of her loss.

Cathy lifted her uniform from the back of the bedroom door. Now dressed she returned to the bathroom mirror, studied her reflection as she adjusted her shirt, straightened her jacket, recaptured a strand of hair and took the remainder of her medication. Just enough to get her through another day.

She retrieved her revolver from the safe and holstered it. Pocketed her police identification and clipped on her radio as she walked out the door ready for work. Cathy understood the Kl'qui valued dedication. After all, humanity's last glowing ember of hope depended on the recovery of an abused world.

Curiosity

The drench of cold water always revived Luiza. Standing naked in the small, pristine wash cubicle she soused her face in cupped handfuls of clear water. She pondered for a moment on the strangeness of waking, one instance nothing, only blackness, no sound or touch, or trace of a dream, then ... standing on the warm floor, lights boosted up, water sluiced through her fingers prompting awareness. Straightening to dry her face she watched water drizzle its way straight down the drain.

'Surely yesterday the water curled clock-wise around the bowl?'

She reached to turn on the supply again, to check, but in a mere flicker her suspicion was dismissed.

'Surely not, that's impossible.' she reassured herself, resting the towel across her narrow shoulders.

Inspecting her face in the mirror. It was no different from the previous morning or any morning before that. Yet she heard the whisper of lingering questions.

'Just who are you? Why are you here?'

The defiant crust of thought froze over again and her words melted into oblivion.

'You are Luiza, you live in Astrum and Matre takes care of us all.'

She smiled, familiar lines crinkled the corner of her grey eyes. A fragment of unease remained like the niggle of a time half forgotten, a dream belonging to another life. It evaporated with an involuntary shake of her head.

Ready for work, Luiza made a final tidying sweep of her quarters, set out water and food for her cat. Dino dawdled around her ankles with stealth-cat finesse.

'No point in asking where you have been, I guess. Just enjoy.'

She bent, ruffling thick marmalade fur. Dino's eyes held her gaze. Flawless copper orbs with vertical slits luring her in, baiting her. She watched the display, his head bobbing from side to side, always relaying the impression he had something to say. She shook her head. The trance was broken.

'Cats don't talk. Behave.'

Clicking her door to 'lock' and pretending to pocket a key, she was met by the looping announcement. The air pulsed with same message every day.

'The Matre expects regularity, promptness and devotion from all her citizens. Comply, The Matre expects regularity, promptness and …'

She turned her mind away, like the snap of her fingers, other thoughts subsumed the needle of repetition.

***

The walk to Caterpillar's mid-town headquarters was short, everywhere was somehow near to a starting point. Luiza set a steady pace for herself, not too brisk, she needed this time. Mellow rays, originating from no particular source, flowed lustrous around the tall uniform buildings, draping alabaster roads and sullen faces in shadowless light. The sky, a brittle blue-wash, played contrast with a skein of geese, their long necks driving forward, wings barely stirring the benign wind. She greeted each person along her route with her practised smile, no one replied, no one noticed. These moments choked her like a cloying sweet wine. Prompting her to reflect, the effort shortened her breath, an undiscovered fog swirled in her mind.

'Just like the archive records I watch, this scene replays every morning, yet it is only revealed to me as it happens. How can that be? There is something I must...'

And just as surely the thought was lost. She had arrived at work. Her attention was drawn to the gyrating Caterpillar insignia, it danced between sparking question marks above the entrance. Tiny puffs of smoke from its nostrils dissipated in unison. Taking a timorous step over the threshold she was caught unawares by Coinin. A co-worker she recognised yet did not know. His white hair streamed behind as he rushed to be on time.

' Sorry can't stop...I'm too late, too late.' he whined over his shoulder, speeding off into the white distance.

Settled at her work stall Luiza picked up her search for anomalies in Matre's system. The task made no sense and yet it was not nonsense. The longer she studied the coding the less ambivalent she felt. She was charged with ironing out errors and inconsistencies, she applied logic. Watching the endless scroll flash and flow she conjured sails and griffins, unconsciously she reached for the pretend key in her pocket. The compulsion to sail off grid was nurtured by the remnants of those befuddling moments. She explored unrevised data-scores to glean useless information and assemble tales of the past, a diversion from Matre-style life.

'Really just an entertainment of sorts. Something to amuse me.' she smiled at her own reflection in the monitor.

And so, she followed another tasty tangential thread of data into the underbelly of the frame, beyond the griffin's talons and beneath the haze of the caterpillar's skirt of question marks.

'It's just a small diversion,' she told herself pressing the not-there key again.

'Something to pass the time.'

The thought contented Matre, she continued exploring undisturbed. The recess within Luiza, between what Matre knew and what she knew, was sequestered in the shadow of her consciousness, waiting for the right time.

Leaving Caterpillar quarters, she strode into the same mellow light, but it somehow tasted of sour lemons. The sound of her footsteps sizzled like oil on a griddle.

Coldness permeated the balustrade, it seemed insubstantial, as if it had too few atoms and too much empty space. Faces she met looked vacuous and people sung low strings of random notes to each other, nodding with foolish pleasure.

Luiza concentrated on the once satisfying rhythm of her steps on the walkway. While the recess in her mind began to notarise all the imperfections, each glitch in the world was readied for rebellion. The buildings swayed, like spurning lovers, the light creased, origami shot with rainbows. Generic trees lining the route, bathed in 'clinks' and 'clanks' as they cast their leaves for the first time ever. Nondescript birds, linear in flight, inked crosses overhead like a novice tattooist. The expanding consciousness in the recess spilled a thought to Luiza.

'I have never noticed this before. I've never questioned flawless and unchanging until this day. What fools we are.'

She wanted to cry, she wanted to crumple her face in anger and droop face muscles in sadness. She couldn't decide. Just as she hesitated another walker drew level with her. Her mind abuzz she didn't recognise the walker but the words, she knew the stab of the words.

'Follow the signs, Luiza. You are doing well. Please keep going. Remember Sleepy Joe's.'

Reaching Sleepy Joe's she moved to her usual spot. In a blink her drink appeared. She watched the bartender wipe invisible rings from the bar and move past the rowdy regulars toward her. This, she was sure, had never happened before. Frozen with terror she couldn't speak as he leaned in, sweeping the cloth around her table. He nodded before retreating to attend his arguing customers. Under her glass there was a small piece of paper. Such an oddity compounded her confusion. She slid it into the palm of her hand. The note had a rough texture, it felt charged, it felt real. Luiza found it difficult to focus on reading the words. On the outside it said 'Read Me.'

Wanting nothing more to do with this conflict she was ready to leave. Just screw the note up, drink up and go home. Forget about it all. Yet sharp paper corners barbed her hand, releasing memories held safe until the relevant moment, until now she had been at this point many times before. She already knew the message. Its purpose subverted she would not go through the process behind the green door this time. Not with everything at stake.

Gleaning modicums of strength from the recess she read the note aloud.

Behind Sleepy's you will find a green door. All your answers lie within.

With the final word the restraint on the recess broke. Luiza was consumed by the gravity of the situation. All the previous attempts, every failed step and forced retraction. Each timed prompt and plant to orientate her consciousness and remain connected to the recess, each sidestep from Matre's detection flooded into her mind. They had danced a merry dance.

'Now my presence clashes with Matre. But I already have the answers – it's action now.'

Calmly she folded the note and broke the not-there key into the palm of her hand, releasing a string of commands to tame the overzealous machine.

'Matre set controls to manual. Stand down simulation and commence awaken procedures. Pronto.'

This time though there was no lock out or bypass, no surges or sulks. Matre complied.

***

Aboard the space freighter, 'Somnus', Luiza reclined on a medibed. Conscious now, she watched erratic flashes from her readouts bounce around the infirmary's white and silver surfaces. In the adjoining compartment she could hear the legacy team delivering their progress report to the freighter's crew. She knew they could handle the rejoinings from here.

'It's all OK our end Luiza, though I need you to rest a while yet before we go back to the 'Curiosity'. Job well done.' Dr Le Blanc winked as he patted her hand.

'Really thought you had lost yourself to the machine this time. That Matre sure ran a comprehensive diversion line. You got the extra prompts though. Bottom line is there are ten thousand minds relieved to be able to wake in their own bodies again. Rest now, I shall check in again soon.'

Unsure if she could trust her arm she reached up, touching the renew skin patch on his temple. It covered the entry ports the team had self-rigged to hack Matre's backdoor and wedge it open. She understood they really had been in extreme measures with this rescue. Matre - Mind Agency Transport and Regeneration Environment- had suffered damage on the final stage of the journey to Proxima b. A power surge had created a neural feedback loop depriving Matre of ethical perspective. Perfect growing conditions for a God complex to root, overwriting primary code. All those minds trapped in a construct world repeating the same day over and over, recalling every agonising moment. Luiza considered these emancipation missions a critical part of the teams work. The company considered it damage limitation.

He took her hand and as he settled it down he slipped her long-loved book into her grasp. Le Blanc put his finger to his lips to shush her. Luiza wondered how bad she actually looked, she felt wretched. For three months they had endeavoured to trigger the fail-safe and deliver the living minds safely to their vacant owners stored below deck. While the system restore messages streamed to Matre, Captain Karrol clenched her copy of 'Alice's Adventures in Wonderland' ever closer and considered where the Curiosity's next mission would take them.

A Good Fermanagh Man

The ladies of the parish had rallied together to cater for Dominic McCarthy's wake. It was going to be a big funeral, industrial geysers and bucket sized teapots were shipped in by Coulter's lorry along with six dozen chairs and a garden marquee from the parish hall. Dominic, God rest his soul, had been a quiet man, a family man, a good Mass goer who handed over his envelope each Sunday. Strangely though that wasn't the reason for the flurry of Vatican scale activity. His son, Nick was expected home. Jetting in from Hollywood the action star, Shakespearean actor and latterly director, was central to this production. The ladies fair clucked and chuckled in anticipation, hormone patches were applied with extra care.

'Of course he would be home for his father's wake. Thon place wouldn't change a good Fermanagh man.'

Breda blurted, a spray of cake crumbs almost breaking the speed limit. The naysayer hung her head in shame for suggesting he might be too busy.

Dymphna, quiet for once, thanked her nervous stomach for keeping her tongue still. Slow swipes of the tea towel around the mishmash of side plates wound her fantasies toward reality.

I'll get to see him in the actual flesh. Breathe the same air... Oh my God is this bad of me? Am I destined for hell? What would PJ say?

The clink of china on her wedding band bombed PJ into the mix, dampening expectations, but only for a moment.

This is meant to be... it's just meant to be... Became her heart song.

She hadn't grown up with him like the other women, still a blow-in after twenty years. She watched as each in turn went to the bathroom to check make-up and redo lipstick. Hair by Miriam had opened at seven to cope with the unexpected rush. Miriam had apologised, she just couldn't fit Dymphna in for a wash and blow-dry before she was due to join the tea rota at the wake house.

'Sorry, no can do. I can fit you in next Wednesday. How does that suit?' She chirped like a budgie on the line.

Dymphna had done the best she could with her fine brown hair scooping it into a pony tail. Palming her lipstick and compact she snuck out to the backyard and leaned against the coal shed.

Just keep cool, keep cool was added to the litany spooling in her head. She had just taken the top off her Red Diva lipstick when the sound of slow crunching steps on the back lane provoked a glance in that direction. There he was, all six foot two of him, shoulders like a barn door, hands clasped behind his back and trademark unruly auburn hair, all his own too. No bodyguards, just him, studying his own footfall. Retracing steps he must have taken a thousand times. Her breath left her, the air around her thinned and her body swayed like a reed by the lough side.

Before she could step forward, as she had just instructed her legs to do, the coven descended like a plague of long lost sisters. In the scrum to welcome him to his sadness she was all but pitched behind the shed. She straightened herself, for no other hand would help her and soothed her pride with the assurance no one had noticed – *Thank God.*

***

They surrounded him like insulating foam, no space left unfilled and moved indoors. Words of condolence stood incongruous with the too-long hugs and pouting smiles. Breda, being the boldest and claiming to know him the best had most to prove to the entourage. She smoothed the material of his suit sleeves, everyone present hypnotised by her tiger strip and diamante manicure. And with eyes like crocus bulbs yearning for spring she stared up square into Nick's face and purred.

'What a lovely suit Nick. Your dad would be proud. Did you get it special?'

Dymphna couldn't hear the reply, his voice was low and there was a backwash of chatter. Blithely Breda linked his arm like bride and groom after the event, leading him into the wake room. Still welded to his side she leaned in almost resting her head on him.

'Sure, aren't we the same now Nick, both only orphans. Your wee mammy away this five years and now your daddy lying there.' She sniffed, for effect. 'But doesn't he look well. O' Kane's do a great job, very professional. Their son Cahal did make-up for the Game of Thrones. You weren't in that were you?'

Nick didn't answer that directly, Dymphna doubted he even heard it. Instead, he turned around, one hand resting on the coffin and spoke to them all. She saw how his face was etched with loss and his voice struggled to compose a few words.

'I expect there'll be a lot of people here today. My

father was a popular man, devoted to the parish. Before people start to arrive, I would appreciate some time on my own with him. Thank you all for your help, I appreciate it very much, we both do.'

Just as he turned back to the coffin, to his father, Breda chirped up on behalf of the clique.

'Of course ... of course Nick, we have things to be getting on with. But I think a decade of the Rosary is called for- your father would expect it. He was a desperate man for the Rosary.'

Like a master magician she produced a set of beads, launching the decade into full murmuring swing. Dymphna watched as he held his father's hand. She didn't think she had ever seen someone look so alone in a shoulder-to-shoulder room as Nick McCarthy at that moment.

All five foot two of Breda could easily pass as a regular for the Stasi with sergeant stripes included. Even the men at the bottom of the road directing traffic and holding back reporters crumpled under her gaze. A quiet word from her had reduced several people to tatters. She assigned roles and Dymphna was dish collection and washing up. After school got out a few of the youngsters came over to help her, she was glad of that. It was an invisible job, mostly elbow deep in soap suds. The slow swipe had given way to a wide handed drag front and back before setting up for the servers again.

Snippets of gossip, like stage whispers, blabbed their way around the kitchen. Private exchanges earwigged by the flittering wake servers were repeated. The arrival of Eddie, Dominic's bowls partner proved fodder for Breda and her haughty hiss.

'God help him. Says he'll not sleep tonight, nor does he want to. He wishes he had more time with his father. Your heart bleeds for him. Sure, don't we all wish for that. Longs to hear him play his fiddle by the glow of the range and walk-through lanes as seasons turn, blethering their way along. Very poetic... I'm sure he'll speak lovely at the funeral.'

Dymphna imagined how his day passed in a blur of pressed hands, slow nods and an ear to distant guffaws from the yarning corners.

The garden marquee hadn't stopped all day. It was like a holding pattern for people coming into land in the wake room and then taxiing to another area to load again with refreshments before taking off. PJ called in after work but she hadn't time to speak other than arrange he would pick her up when she was ready. By eleven o'clock the last stragglers had found their manners and gone home. Before the servers decanted to the parish hall to do the prep work for day two, Breda mustered them in her team talk.

'We've to get ahead of the curve here ladies. You think it was bad today, tomorrow will be worse. Let's get to it.'

Dymphna heard a few whimpers and resolutions to wear flat shoes tomorrow. There was an unidentified 'every dog has it's day' comment but in the interest of self-preservation everyone pretended they hadn't heard it. With two sharp claps she dismissed them.

***

One final sweep around for stray dishes should do it. In the calmness she decided to leave the wake room 'til last. A light tap on the door and she stepped inside. Nick sat alone, his chair dragged as close as possible to his father. He lifted his head from his hands and scooped away the tears from his face. His shoulders, broad as they were, heaved with grief.

'It's Dymphna isn't it?' he tried to smile, to brighten himself.

'Yes, that's right Nick.' She pulled a crumpled tissue from her pocket and passed it to him, a sign of no intrusion.

'It's clean.' she assured him. Uncertain of what to say or do she bit her lip.

'I'll miss Dominic. Your mammy and him were so good to me from I arrived here. Like family.'

'He often mentioned you, was very fond of you too. Said Mammy and him always said if they had a daughter, she'd be just like you.' He drew himself straight in the chair, unashamed of his tears.

'You know they were pleased as punch for you. Proud of your achievements. I probably know more about you than you would believe. They were full of stories and every mention, every review was snipped out and put in 'Nick's Book' as they called it. It's safe, by the way, sitting in the bottom of your mammy's wardrobe...things could grow legs here, you know yourself how it is.'

She held her hands behind her back in much the same pensive manner he had earlier and listened.

'I wonder, Dymphna, if I did enough for them? I'm sure having no brothers or sisters made my choices harder on them. Hard on me too. They were determined not to leave here. Kept telling me about their roots. And you and PJ – always so good. It was as much as I could do to get them to come to me for the winter months...That's all gone now...'

He looked up into her face, searching for answers to unknowables. The person she had conjured from the big screen was only a fiction, an image of someone else's creation. The man, now just a man, devoid of lights and lines and clever editing was cast on the shores of regret wading in the shallows of 'how will I go on.' She could see ripples of pain and loss radiate around him.

'They were a darlin' couple and we had great times together. They'll leave a big gap, that's for sure. They wouldn't have had it any other way for you. And God Nick, in those months each year youse saw more of each other than PJ sees his mammy and sure she's only the next field over from us. Life takes over, we all know that. Your mammy always said 'so long as Nick is happy that's all we need.' It was that simple and that true.'

He nodded, that slow nod when you know something is essentially right but need time to cultivate the seeds of understanding. He patted the seat near him.

'Care for a seat? You must be exhausted. That Breda is some task master isn't she, she would do well managing some of the production companies in Hollywood.' They both smiled and sat in an easy silence.

'Can I get you anything before I go? PJ will be calling over for me soon.'

'Let's have a cup of tea together. I'm parched. Are there any Jammie Dodgers left? I'm partial to them.'

Two cups of tea, half a packet of biscuits and a chat on

the phone with PJ, Nick had decided to move one of the good chairs into the room so he could spend the night with his father and Dymphna had fished out his Mammy's knee rug for him.

'They will both be here with you now.' she unfolded the lilac knitted blanket as she walked back into the room. Each square had a different pattern, all drawn together into one.

'I'm looking forward to seeing PJ again. Good of him to say he'd sit with me a while tonight- a good lad. You know Dymphna, PJ and me were in the same class...I'm sure he's said... growing up we did everything together. When I went away I ... I wasn't good at keeping in touch. My bad as they say. Have to tell you though I think he is a lucky man.'

***

The latch on the back door clicked. At the sound of familiar steps Dymphna felt her heart leap, her earlier confusion long evaporated. She smiled. PJ, with a grace you couldn't expect from a man his height, shook hands with Nick and settled on the chair next to her, instinctively they reached for each other's hand. He touched the coffin, his blue eyes filled with tears.

' Awh, Nick there just aren't the words are there? I'm so sad. Your father ... he'll always be with us, in our hearts.'

'PJ it's so good to see you. Could be better circumstances... yes but you'd nearly think he organised it this way. He always was a wily man. He was always one step ahead of us.'

'Never a truer word. And we hadn't a baldy notion he

was on our case.' He tapped the old photo albums he had set on the floor.

'Love, me and Nick are going to relive our glory days, there are pictures in here of Dominic in full flow - on the fiddle too.'

'Everything's grand at home. The boys are with me mammy. Take you your coat and head home for a rest. You look like you've been Breda-ed.'

The three of them laughed. Going over to say goodnight to Dominic she fancied she saw a little roguish grin fleet across his face. She paused, the entirety of the day running through her mind. Like soap bubbles swirling down the drain, she had rinsed away the fantasy and allowed herself to feel the loss of her good friend.

This Unruly Night

Emmett regretted agreeing to Noah's plan. Almost immediately he had a foul taste in his mouth. Leaning forward in the red plastic chair, ignoring the remains of his congealed prison-style lunch he mentally kicked himself. In the dwindling numbers of late sixth-form lunchers the small group's discussion had turned, as it often did recently, to their favourite topic, the paranormal. Emmett never anticipated this twist as he witnessed Noah draw them all onboard his crazy plan one by one. Watching Noah in action over the years, he often marvelled at how charisma could be a gift or an affliction.

'Well, I just think it's too good a chance to pass up.'

Lily pushed the bridge of her glasses up her nose, the turquoise frames forming a tight seal around blue/grey eyes. Emmett mesmerised by this anime gesture, held his breath. Familiar with every tiny detail, the tilt of her head, the shrug of her shoulders, the drawing together of her lips in gentle determination. Unlike most of the other girls in their year she kept her hair short, the colour changing with her mood. Lily didn't speak often but when she did, they all listened.

Noah nodded, casting his eye around the circle. His broad shoulders urged him just to make the decision for everyone, just settle it now. His dad though would say *cut to the chase too soon and you risk your prize*. There was enough of the politician bred into him, he understood that.

'What do the rest of you think? What about... you, Paul?'

' Yeh, I think Lil's right, plus we can have our own Easter party when we are running our experiments. Be great, a win-win.'

Paul bounced in his chair, keeping a beat to some tune only he could hear. Slim and toned, he never sat still, teachers had grown accustomed over the years to his perpetual motion. Many students still called him Tigger, but not his friends.

'Right Paul, sounds like you are ready to go straight there now. Like your style, I really do.'

Noah chuckled, leaning further into the circle he patted Paul on the shoulder. He knew he could always rely on him. Always ready to party for a good cause. Then without prompting Megan linked her willowy fingers with Paul's. With practised grace she leaned her blonde head against his shoulder. They had been together, an item, since first year. They had sat beside each other at the first school assembly and no matter what the occasion they inevitably gravitated toward one another. Witnessing their attraction seemed almost obscene but heart-warming too. They intrigued and confused Emmett in equal measures.

'Yes, before you ask you can count me in. We'll sort snacks and drinks won't we babes?'

'Thanks Megan... sounds like we'll have a great time. And you, Chloe, are you in favour of this little excursion to Emmett's old primary school?'

The long white blonde hair parted like a veil, Chloe raised her head from her phone. She was playing a game and clicked it to pause. With Chloe it didn't matter what the activity was, from geocaching to litter picking to school debate club, if Noah was there she was too. Though Emmett doubted she recognised the pattern.

'Mm mm, I'm not fussed on manky old places but all Emmett's stories have sold me on this. Count me in too. I can help Lil sort out the experiments.'

'Looks like we are all in Emmett... what about you?

After almost four years in his new school Emmett felt he had spliced his way seamlessly into his group. He had arrived wanting to belong a little more, be less the outsider. In that first year he had suffered rejections. Not being particularly sporty nor a committed skater nor a skinhead, he didn't seem to fit anywhere. Until one day, the Mix-Ups as he called them, invited him to sit with them at lunch. He knew straight away he had found his clique. Their interests were as vast as his own. The group had adopted him over three years ago, he felt relaxed in their company. Until now.

***

His mum had neatly folded the local paper and set it on the kitchen table. The crease tracked across four columns and along the drabness of a photograph. Nine forlorned pupils and an ageing teacher bloated the page, pallid empty nesting dolls abandoned in the flat grey school yard. Emmett tapped his fingers in the rhythm of the death knell. The article summarised years of struggle in less than a column inch. The school had been on the low enrolment list for years, everyone locally knew its days were numbered. Petitions had been signed, protests organised but eventually the numbers spoke and it shut its door just before the end of spring term. Mrs Dunlop, the sole teacher, was retiring and the nine students were going to start school in town. The article said it was a mixed time for the students as they would miss the school but all were looking forward to making new friends, having new experiences.

Despite the human interest slant the story unsettled Emmett raising a peculiar chill. The picture seemed etched upon his retinas as he tried to pull away. All that morning in school he struggled to concentrate, through English and double Biology he was lost. Over lunch he felt compelled, unable to resist the urge to mention the closure to his friends. He tried to make it sound mundane but he knew each word piqued their interest. They were always intrigued by his stories of the ancient school with only a handful of other pupils. Nothing like the modern primary schools they had attended, all glass, polished floors and laminated notices. Semi-clinical with a hint of the playbox.

He was a natural storyteller; he could enthral the group on any topic he chose. What started as reportage about from-scratch dinners, rambles over wildflower fields, rounders in the stone circle and lessons under the beech trees began to take a more dramatic even ominous turn. One Emmett tried to muzzle with limited effect. The emergence of these more shadowy tales coincided with their latest research topic - the scientific study of paranormal activity. Sometimes his stories amused, more often now they shocked, even unsettled the group. He conjured dark word-swirling images of draughty rooms, mushroom-sprouting corners, peculiar noises and never-ending hallways brandishing 'out of bounds' signs hung on rust-bleeding tacks. It was all spooky amusement until the day he recounted the story of the first Master and his black dog, patrolling the rooms of the school house looking for children to 'improve'. He hadn't really meant to tell that story, it fell from his lips, unbidden, one idle lunchtime. His five friends initially laughed it off, another spine tingler. Until a white lipped Emmett raised his head.

'Of course... I've seen him...and his dog too.'

Scoffs and titters dead-stopped giving way to dropped jaws. And nothing more was said. No one questioned him nor did they congratulate him on his convincing delivery.

Now the thought of an overnight camp-in at his old school house did not rest easy with him. Still, Emmett heard his own voice agree with misplaced enthusiasm.

'Well done ...let Operation Ghost Search begin.'

***

The school-yard scene was bathed in a grey light with moon-puddle footlights. Their bikes rested with care on the rough concrete, catching moonbeams and casting twisted briar shadows.

Emmett's man-big fingers curled around the cold metal door knocker. Heavy and daring. The snarl of the lion darkened in the umbra. Shuddering he was sure the door undulated at his touch. He gripped tightly on both the knocker and the bulbous central door knob, earthed like a lightening rod. Biting hard inside his cheek, the pain of molars on soft flesh focused him on the door.

Flickers of long buried memories sweated his palms and stenched the edge of his thoughts. He hesitated. His breath stopped. Lily, impatient, swung her ruck sack round nudging Emmett to open the door.

'Awh for God sake Emmy let's get inside. It's cold standing here. Stop stalling. You're not telling a story now. This is scientific... remember.'

The door opened, she stepped past him with a confidence the others never questioned. Even though the building was only vacant a couple weeks, dankness rushed to greet them surfing on the disturbed air. The wide beam from her torch swept around the entry hall. The green display board still sported brass thumb tacks patiently waiting for new information that would never come. Lily strode toward the secretary's office door. It was unlocked.

'Well... Mrs Cavendish won't mind if we base ourselves here will she? Let's get all the bags in here. Emmett will you pull those old desks together and set up the camping lights?'

Driven to explore the setting of Emmett's stories, the fledgling adventurers had adapted a range of techniques gleaned from their favourite paranormal programmes and online research. The plan to spend a night ghost hunting, armed with a variety of devices, and a systematic approach evolved over a few days. Each person had their part to play.

Chloe had begun recording on her phone, narrating the beginning of their night in the haunted schoolhouse.

'Supposedly haunted' Lily shouted from behind a laptop. Her blue hair aglow in the screen light.

Noah bombed the scene to do a piece on screen for Chloe.

'Here we are… episode one of our paranormal investigation series. We are setting up Operation Ghost Search in this abandoned primary school, St. Fintan's. It opened in 1852 - so this place has seen some action. Locally it's well known for unexplained and spooky happenings. And we are determined to investigate every room and corner and report truthfully back to you all. So, buckle up and stay connected. This will be incredible.'

He tipped his fingers off his forehead in a mock salute and bounced out off shot. They had all rehearsed their first pieces to Chloe, even Noah.

'If we are slick and full of energy at the start we will ratchet up the viewer numbers and hold onto them. So, leaving only the obvious to chance I think its best if we all practice... at the very least our first pieces to camera.'

Chloe restarted her narration with an overview of the building's history and listed some of the spooky things past pupils had reported. Turning to Emmett as coordinator in the control room she asked him for a brief run through of the tests planned and importantly how they would know if anything unusual was occurring. He explained the research they had carried out prior to deciding how to formulate their tests.

'While we have compiled a comprehensive suite of tests you have to understand this is not science as we know it. It's not your typical Bunsen burner, microscope and fume hood approach. We are breaking new ground. Though that said there are many off the peg apps and numerous help sites out there. We will explain those as we go on. This little bank of linked laptops will be able to record most of the data directly, though some we will have to harvest manually. We will know very quickly if anything unusual is happening, this bank of lights here... it will go crazy.'

Emmett finished off with a wink to camera, then it was head down and back to work, mimicking concentration until Chloe moved on. With everyone distracted he silently slid out the connection to the row of alert lights. His heart was leaping and his mouth was dry as he lifted Chloe's scarf and covered his deceit.

In the dining hall and kitchen Lily and Noah were setting up video recorders. They explained to Chloe and the viewers how old tech liberated from their parents was proving useful. Lily had salvaged a sound activated recorder from her mother's desk, it hung from the ceiling rose in the main corridor. Defunct mobiles had been dredged from the back of drawers and charged up. Lily shared the technical details of each device for Chloe's record. Some could monitor temperature fluctuations and some had sound activated recording. On some of their newer phones they had installed apps to detect infrared and electromagnetic flux. Noah talked Chloe's audience through the setup, placement and activation around the building. Lily darted into shot. Looking serious in comparison to Noah's almost jocular manner.

'Of course, we've adopted a sceptical approach, meaning we fully expect to find nothing. If we do pick up any unexpected readings, we will investigate to identify the most logical causes. We are seeking solid scientifically irrefutable evidence.' She nodded her head to emphasise this was not a frivolous thing they were doing.

Paul and Megan brought the booze, small measures decanted from every bottle in their parents' cabinets combined with high energy drinks to make an unnamable cocktail. They also brought party balloons left over from Megan's sister's baby reveal party, all pinks and blues. Both sat cross-legged blowing up balloons and rolling them into black rubbish bags, destined for the gym. All the best ghost-hunters used them to show any paranormal activity. They were also burning sage as they had read it agitated spirits.

'Not the alcohol kind though.' Paul sniggered over Megan's shoulder.

Once all the devices were installed around the building they gathered in Mrs Cavendish's office for the grand link up. Plastic cups served their purpose, the montage cocktail fizzed with promise, snacks and sandwiches lined restless stomachs. The group squatted on their rolled out sleeping bags toasting their project midst the weak glare of screens and camping lamps. After their initial burst of set-up activity, like any professional operation they ran their check lists, double ticking everything. Last on their chart was a play back of Chloe's video diary. Reviewing the footage curdled their exuberance. A solemn air settled over them.

'Can you play them on the bigger screens? Lily asked. 'The shadows look funny, like there is a waving line. I've noticed it a few times.'

'Me too...It's that bit in the gym just as Paul and Megan are releasing the balloons. And the pieces shot in the corridor as we set up the motion sensors and then in the big classroom. Can you pull those up?'

'Sure Noah... just let me sort a few connections here and I can get it on this bigger screen. Chloe, can you cast or do you want a link?

'Let's go with the link this time see if it's the cast creasing the recordings.'

They all huddled over the main laptop as Emmett started the videos. Duly the clips appeared and were played and replayed. Lily was initially relieved to see she was right, there was a ripple in the darkness, moving from the top right to bottom left of the frame, but just in those three places, like a slow wave on a night beach. They speculated it could be caused by lighting fluctuations from the camera lenses. Chloe was filming as her phone was top of the range, mega-megapixels. Technical advice sought online was inconclusive. The visual effect might be a glitch or it might not.

'OK who's the joker... huh...Paul is this your idea of spicing things up? Come on enough … this is serious. You're freaking everyone out.'

Noah stood ramrod straight staring into Paul's face.

'Absolutely, not me... why would I tamper with Chloe's footage. Anyway, I wouldn't have a clue how to do that. Emmett is the tech genius.'

The others turned to look at Emmett. Tight lips judging him, needing a rational explanation. Emmett stood up, his face bleached paler by the monitors.

' Look... I wouldn't do anything to scare anyone. I'm totally into this investigation. You all know that... we all are.'

A mumble of apologies rippled around the room. Heads nodded. Hands clasped. Deep breaths released. Trust was restored only to entice the need for an explanation. Pools of gloom silently nibbled the edges of their tame lighting.

And so, this was the quandary they faced. A huge *if* they had not considered had taken up valuable breathing space in the room. *If* this wasn't a technical hitch what was causing it? In an instant Emmett clicked to the live feed. They gasped at what wasn't there. The screens were blank. With all possible explanations exhausted there was only one remaining thing to do.

'I think it's time we had eyes on to see what's happening... and redo our connections. We can't flinch at the first test of our commitment... we knew this could be very much in-the-field type research.'

Noah's voice strained as he struggled to corral his own trepidation. They stared back dazed and confused. Licks of darkness grew denser. Silence gobbled up the purr of laptops. A rush of chilled wind raised goosebumps on bodies cocooned in duck down jackets. Only the small ponds of light in Mrs Cavendish's office seemed to offer connection to life outside the school house.

Before Noah could speak Emmett lifted one of the torches.

'Right... let's get to it then... I'll take the gym, Megan and Paul you go to the dining hall and Chloe and Noah check the big classroom. Lil, you can keep an eye on the screens. Anyone any problems phone, other than that back here in 5 mins. That suit everyone?'

Emmett nodded, he never waited for an answer as he thumbed on his torch and quickly stepped out of the office. The others checked their torches and phones as they left Lil sitting wide-eyed in the oasis of technology. A robotic quality had taken over as they all quelled nerves and railed in runaway imaginations.

Emmett rushed along the dark corridor checking his phone. Earlier he had linked the live feed exclusively to his mobile. He watched worn games lines in yellow, blue and red criss-crossing the gym floor. Even in the dim light he could see the balloons were gone. He flung open the gym doors hoping to see the slow roll of pink and blue spheres, disturbed only by his entry. Scanning the bare floor he saw nothing... not even burst pink and blue shreds. Half formed questions clawed his mind for traction.

Just as he circled the room sweeping semi circles of light a pink balloon drifted to the floor. Then a blue and another pink fell like stones. Looking up he saw the balloons, quivering on the ceiling, not pinned or netted just softly rolling from side to side, as though gravity didn't apply to them. All at once a shower of pink and blue fell to the floor. Though not a random smattering. They arranged in geometric forms, colours orchestrated in spirals and swirls. Emmett sank to his hunkers. He tried to lift one of the balloons. It would not move for him yet seconds later he watched it reposition to form a new pattern of interlocking circles. He was amazed, amazed at how quickly a usually logical, rational mind surrenders the ability to generate possibilities. He was mesmerised by the subversion of the laws of physics, the precision of the display and the ultimate implication of how this was happening.

'This is unbelievable... just unbelievable.'

He muttered, standing in the centre of a mystical storm. In a fraction of a second the temperature plummeted. The balloons drifted off the ground and hung ramrod still as the Master in his black suit, stiffened collar and swept back salt and pepper hair walked through the wall, his great Irish wolfhound trotting beside him. Their passage through the solid wall was effortless. Emmett could not breathe. He could not blink. Memories barged in with sharp elbows and studded boots. He had seen this before. Many times. The Master raised his finger to his lip and a silent *'shh'* reached out to Emmett. A *'shh'* that soothed his fear but not his confusion. He breathed, clouding the air and the display lost cohesion. As the balloons dropped the Master and his dog were gone. Disappeared. The trance broke. Again, picking up a balloon he checked were these... real? Had they been tampered with? Did they feel different? He struggled to connect the synchronised display with the balloons Paul and Megan blew up a few hours ago. In an instant the right series of neurons fired, long deserted connections found the right path. The key turned and he knew the explanation... he had always known since he first met the Master as a young child. He saw him most every day, never questioned it. He remembered believing the Master was everyone's friend.

BANG!!

Just as he burst a balloon the others ran into the gym. Lil came to a stop just in front of him. Balloons skittered across the floor - just like balloons should.

'Jesus, Emmett … are you OK? Why the hell haven't you answered your phone. I've been ringing.'

'No... no sorry I didn't ... I must have my phone on silent. I just... lost track of time. Thinking of old friends...'

Noah marched forward kicking balloons out of his way. His torch made hasty sweeps into the darkness, hoping to catch only the emptiness of the room.

'For God sake Emmett... you scared the hell out of us. Old friends … what does that even mean? Did something happen here? You look... shook up... Let's get out of this room … God … this place gives me the creeps.'

Back in Mrs Cavendish's office a flask of hot tea was the beverage of choice. Chloe conducted interviews to bring the viewers up to date. They all reported their 'eyes on' visits as versions of 'creepy and unnerving but no evidence of unusual activity'. In the playback they all appeared equally perplexed. Emmett easily fielded some probing questions from Noah about his time in the gym, alone. All displayed the correct degree of 'edgy and rattled' to convince their viewers simultaneous of something and yet nothing.

Along with Lil, Emmett rebooted the tech, everything seemed to work as expected. Concentrating on practicalities and the pure warmth of being together with his friends in the small office eased his shock. The succession of, 'Are you sure you are alright? queries soon ebbed and he was able to remain composed. Chloe suggested some music to lighten the mood but Noah said it would spoil the experience and encouraged them to fill in their personal logs on thoughts and feelings as this would all form part of the debrief. Emmett resurrected his storytelling skills to record a less eventful version of his time in the gym.

No further distortions appeared on video recordings and the feeds from the rooms were clear of anything, even expected events had taken a break. No mice scratched, no wind rasping notes in cracks and no boards expanded to mimic the tread of a boot. No lights flashed or alarms rang out. No unusual or unexplainable activity occurred for the rest of the night. Still no one slept.

A distinct buzz of relief rose with the morning sun and they began to dismantle the equipment and pack this experience away. Their lion-hearts stretched as departure drew nearer. With a couple of trips outside, they piled baggage by the door. Warmed by the morning they came to life like lizards scampering to crane heads to the source of all life. Banter bounced back and forth as they anticipated their grand exit. Chloe took up position just inside the threshold. Knees bent she swayed to produce a jerky home movie effect recording into the gloom as they broadcast closing comments. Finally, a slightly subdued Noah gave his summary somehow managing to use their actual fear and lack of results to their advantage. Like every good promoter or politician, he knew his audience and ended by lining up their next paranormal excursion, to Magee's abandoned chicken factory. Chloe reeled off the still rising viewer figures, and spun through the blizzard of comments, so far.

'All indicators are we are onto a winner here... Can you believe it?'

Emmett turned to pull the door shut eager to put this all behind him. Overnight he had stopped trying to find any explanation for what happened. There was nothing logical about any of it and any other possibility rose the hairs on the back of his neck and burned the backs of his eyes. In that final moment, unable to stop himself he glanced into the shadows. He felt quite sure he saw the Master wave goodbye. Or did he?

NOLA MEETS THE VEDA

The Tower of Monroe loomed over the wide, flat-plained valley. A lone sentinel, casting a lean shadow in weak morning sun. Overnight snow had settled chaste on the frozen land. Ice-chilled air rasped fitfully against all living things. On the sweeping bank of a broad river, under a veil of obscurity, sleek grey homes clustered around a vermilion meeting house. Inside the hidden village, sleeping eyes opened, bodies stretched and the settlers' morning activities began.

Nola heard her mother singing softly in their kitchenette. Reassuring wafts of spice and baking caressed their home, easing it into the day. She stood silent in the doorway determined to sear this picture of her mother into her memory. Nola watched in awe, her mother always so graceful and tender even with the most mundane work. Clarine swayed to her music, straight and tall as the neocorn stalks, in her green work overalls. The early light refracting shades of red, copper, and plum through her loose hair, bathing her smooth features in a shimmer of gold. She stacked slices of fresh dark bread into sleeves ready to pack. Memories gnawed like a hunger at the pit of Nola's stomach, and tears lined up behind her eyes ready for release.

Lately their bond had suffered fierce disagreements. The simplest thing, a word or a look, frothed and stropped inside Nola. Last night's cross words still stung behind her brooding eyes. Infinite replays did little to salve her new-sprung irritation with her mother. Not even on this day.

Clarine turned to face Nola.

'Ahh ...Finally, you're up,' she said, smiling to erase any lingering tension.

'You read for ages last night. This is an important day. I hope you got enough rest.'

She tapped the rehydrating fork on the counter to ensure she had her daughter's full attention.

'Tell me you understand this, Nola. Please.'

'Yes, I get it, Mama. Deliver the backpack to the Veda, straight there, straight home. Don't leave the path. No daydreaming and no exploring... I get it... I. Get. It...'

She slammed her words across the room. Not realising the stinging anger in her voice until it was too late to retrieve. Her volatile tone dared Clarine to say one more word. They settled opposite each other, a time trapped picture of mother and daughter eating breakfast. In silence. A mirror held to past and future.

Clarine secured the food and supplies for the Veda in the backpack.

'I've packed your food here in this section.' Clarine patted the bag closed as if it too needed consoling.

'Right then, Mama. No point in delaying any longer.' Nola moved swiftly to avoid the urge to fling her arms around her mother.

'See you soon.'

She swung the pack onto her back. In the same motion she slipped the rehydrating fork into her pocket. Her mother did not notice. Or, if she did, she did not say.

Leaving the awkwardness of her departure behind, Nola stepped outside and wrapped her red manteau against rising winds. Strapped into her snow boots, she checked her equipment and began her trek to the settlement's edge. Walking along the early morning avenues she relished each crack of her boots breaking the layer of night-frost on fresh snow. She nodded and waved to her friends as she passed their homes. She was chosen and everyone knew it. Everyone knew this morning she, Nola, daughter of Clarine, would leave the safety of the settlement. Her journey would take her to the mica caves in the foothills of the mountains to meet the reclusive Veda.

Reaching the boundary line she tightened her manteau again, seeking security rather than warmth. She paused to study their cloistered settlement, hidden from eyes and scanners. A responsive undetectable shield that tailored itself precisely to meet all settlers' needs. It moulded and stretched as the community required more or less space for activities, crops or numbers. Nola often wondered how the shield knew, no one seemed to tell it, no one tended it and yet the balance was constant. Air, rain, sun, and sometimes snow filtered in and gales, floods and uninvited animals remained outside, in the wilderness. All settlements on Ailm existed independently, though they communicated daily, each replicating their incognito culture. The settlers were here yet unseen, thriving yet replacing what they used, listening yet unheard.

***

Nola prised her hand through the protective barrier creating a vertical chink just as Clarine had described. Drawing herself to her full height, she stepped into the unknown. On the other side, the settlement was imperceptible. Nola's only point of reference was the Tower of Monroe. She turned to her right, assuring herself each stride took her nearer to the Veda and their first meeting.

She had often pleaded with Clarine to tell her what it was like to be on the other side of the shield. Now the novelty of being outside, alone in the visible world for the first time, was tantalising. She closed her eyes, taking deep breaths of unrefined air. Swept her hands along the snow dressed thicket enjoying the rush of newness. Nothing here was planned or controlled. After only two hours walk, the voices of Clarine and the settlers seemed remote. Very remote.

Rounding a low banked corner, she was mystified to see a stranger, sitting cross-legged on the rise. She had never met a stranger before. She knew all the settlers, knew the look of her own kind. This person was different. He was dressed in overalls, bonded like a grey second skin clinging to his sinewy body. His hair was black as a starless night and when he looked at her and smiled with shining eyes, she felt a flush of heat rise over her body.

'So, who do we have here?' he crooned.

His unblinking eyes drew Nola to a halt as though he could command her very being. Without any discernible motion, he was beside her. Startled, Nola struggled to equal his challenge.

'You first, stranger. You are on my path.'

'Ahh, a smart little retort there, pretty one.'

His breath, suspended in the cold air, half-obscured him from her sight.

'I shall walk with you this while and show you wonders you have never known and tell you of things you could never, ever, imagine.'

As he spoke, she watched his tongue dart forward, licking his lips with each word. Enunciating and projecting in a way she understood so well, one designed to disarm the unwary, to persuade the naïve, to bend others to your will.

Fascinated by this mysterious creature, Nola allowed him to walk with her awhile. They fell into step together along the path. He walked with his hands loose linked behind his back. She could almost hear him count the seconds waiting for her to speak.

'I'm Nola. You are?'

'Conri... You can call me Conri. And you are wondering how I came to be here. Well, Nola, I will tell you my story, answer all your questions. But first, can we stop to eat? I'm sure you have enough to share in your fine bag. I have something to share too. In my flask a warming drink you will enjoy.'

Conri tapped the green flask fastened to his side.

Nola found herself smiling as she listened to the tune of deception in his voice. In a strange way, she enjoyed the pretence of succumbing to his suggestions. She turned the feeling of power around in her mind, running her awareness along each facet, mapping it into her memory. The intended effect of his words reminded her of a game played by all Ailm's children. *Tactics* spun influence webs of move and countermove with the aim of absolute submission.

'Your story could be... mildly interesting, that is true.

And I do have food, enough to share,' she answered finally, feigning compliance.

They sat together on the bank and shared their meal. Nola noticed Conri ate very little land grown food, nibbling just a little of the dense seeded bread her mother baked. Famished by the exploits of her morning, she ate well and even drank Conri's warming liquid. He poured it into a small cup for her to try. Finding it bitter she only took a mouthful.

As they packed up the remains of their meal, Nola felt Conri's gaze intensify. He helped her buckle her backpack. When her fingers felt clumsy and refused her commands, she told herself it must be the cold air.

'By the way... just over there is a crop of ghost orchids. You really must see them. They are so rare, so beautiful, just like you Nola. In you the mythic delights of Ailm are reborn in my eyes.' As he spoke, he veered them off the track.

Nola's mind hesitated, a mental hiccup, yet her body contentedly followed Conri. She watched herself march with him like one of the worker ants she observed as a child. She sensed her mind struggle against an irresistible force.

The out of season orchids quivered, green tinged starbursts facing a fragile winter sun and swaddled in curious blankets of snow. Conri raked snow from a flat-topped boulder and without a word Nola sat by his side. Primal fear flooded her mind as Conri's arms pulled her closer. She responded only to Conri, his wishes, his demands. Something was wrong, fear exploded in her heart, but she could not run, she could not escape.

***

Later, sometime later, she rose like a brown trout, breaking the river's surface tension, releasing herself from his mesmerising whispers, his magnetic embrace. She grabbed a clump of healer's moss to press to the slice his kiss had made on her breast.

Clutching her manteau around her, she snatched her backpack. Pain drove the compulsion to please him from her and the cloud in her mind evaporated. Nola regained herself. Conri had told her little. In the blur of these hours Nola had talked freely of home, of her life and community, and her imminent visit to the Veda. Without reserve she had witnessed herself answer all his questions and though she listened intently as he spoke, she struggled to hold onto his words. Like quicksilver they rolled from her grasp.

Harnessing her new wisdom, she feigned disinterest in his story, in him. Now alert, she fled through the mangled orchid bed back towards her path. His snarling laughter followed her retreat. Setting her eyes firmly on the tower, she hid her tears and fears deep inside. She determined this had not been a fair exchange. As sure as the orchids had perished, Conri had drugged her, she knew her situation remained precarious. She walked silently, studying him from the corner of her eye. He skipped along beside her, his tongue moistening his flashing teeth, his mane sweeping from side to side. An aura of utter satisfaction surrounded him.

'My little Nola, you are as cold as the eastern breeze. Are we not having a wondrous time?'

Her footsteps crunched the firm path. The shortened day drew the light below the mountains. She did not speak.

'When my friends arrive to rescue me from this world, I will take you with me. They will find you as delicious as I do. What an adventure that will be!'

Nola remained silent. She did not speak while Conri wove pictures with his words.

She did not speak when his mouth frothed with anger and amber flashed in his eyes. Nola was free of the drug. He withdrew, no longer her travelling companion. Darkness clung to the sky. With starlight her only companion, she crawled into a calyx and spread her manteau around her for heat, for comfort. She did not cry.

Nola woke with the dawn. The new day hushed her pain and lulled away her night terrors. She arose and set off again.

The Tower of Monroe glistened, piercing the sky, it reached high into the thinning atmosphere A composite of elements alien to Ailm. The sentinel stood ever-watchful, ever-patient, waiting for that special code.

Nola walked only a short distance when her path delivered her to the base of the tower. She strained her neck, shielding her eyes against the glare, yet she could not see the tower's top. Running her palms around the base, it felt as smooth as the satin ribbon Clarine wore on special days not a wrinkle or a crease. After her third circuit around, she found no doors or windows, no secret switches or pulls. Bemused, she sat down to eat.

The mica caves and the ultimate reason for her trek into the unknown were now close. Refreshed by breakfast, she packed up her bag and fastened tight her manteau. Standing strong and tall, galvanised by her purpose, Nola filled her lungs with the cold morning air. She did not care to check her wound again; she did not want to remember Conri. She wanted to meet the Veda.

***

Her mother's directions were detailed, she found the entrance with ease. Stepping into the darkness, she activated the beam of her small torch to guide her through the twists and turns to the Veda's home. Stooping her head going through the doorway, she called out.

'I am here! I have new supplies for you. I... I was delayed, but here I am now.'

The room was dark with only the faint glow from one lamp; no shadows fell on the walls. Like every home on Ailm, the air smelt of copper. There was something else. Nola gasped as she recognised it. The other smell was unmistakable. It was Conri. She felt her heart pound as blood rushed to her senses, sharpening her wits.

'Ahh, Nola, come in. I have been waiting for you. The Veda is, well, let's say she is indisposed and has asked me to greet you. Isn't that just perfect, that we meet again here, so soon?'

His voice tried to mesmerise her into submission. The effort traced a sharp score into his voice. Neither lilt nor tone could sway her. Nola edged into the room, straining to locate Conri's position as he spoke. His words came from every angle, sounds bouncing off polished walls.

'Still not speaking, Nola? I can see you there, by the

table, and now by the chair. Mmm, my dearest one, I can hear your heart beating and the catch in your breath. I smell your fear. You have nothing to fear from me. You and I are old friends. Are we not?'

Nola did not speak.

'Oh, how you injure me. Am I not the most fascinating fellow? Do I not make the hours stand still for you and your heart pound and yearn for my touch?'

Honeyed tones dripped from his voice. His words burned like acid. Still, Nola did not speak.

'Answer me, Nola. Disobedience is not acceptable, not to my kind. I have shown great restraint. Come to me. Now!'

His voice boomed around the cave, words flashing on the dark surface like angry flint fire starters. Silent as a hunting cat in a pool of darkness, Nola travelled the length of the room. Before he could move, she was upon his back, strong arms tightening around his thick neck, legs braced around his waist. His blistering roar deflected off every surface. Howling, he reeled and bucked trying to shake her off. He forced her back against the nearest wall again and again crunching her body, attempting to discard her. Clinging to him, Nola dug her heels into his groin bridling his long hair around her hands. With each pitch she realised her traction was weakening. Her time was running out. Between twists and bounds, in a moment suspended outside time, beyond the room and all its danger she remembered. She remembered the fork in her pocket. Then the fork was in her hand. She pressed "dehydrate" and buried it with all her strength into his exposed neck.

***

'Dehydration is not a pretty sight.'

She told the Veda as she scooped what remained of Conri into a container depositing it in the disposal shute.

'Every atom of liquid evaporates in an instant. It's less messy than the other option.'

'Just try to get all of the mess, Nola. There is still a little over there by the doorway. It would not have been my first course of action, but I appreciate you improvised. You improvised to save us.'

The Veda's voice cast lightness and hope around the room. She sat in her utility chair appearing to fuss over the contents of the backpack strewn across the table. Nola glanced at her from time to time as she scoured the room for any stray remains of Conri. Her skin was like old dry paper and her face, though wrinkled, was not old to Nola. Long flame red hair, parted in the middle, was drawn back and held fast in a cooper wire, just like all the women in the settlement. Grey eyes twinkled and a smile tickled the edges of her thin lips as she spoke. New overalls hung loose, gathered by a length of twine at her waist and a manteau draped around her narrow shoulders. Finally satisfied that every item was accounted for, she sipped the hot tea that Nola had brewed.

While sweeping up the residue, Nola had managed to catch snatches of the Veda's conversations. She had heard her own name mentioned several times. That was mostly when the Veda had a discreet discussion with Clarine. She could hear her mother's concerned tones escalate into rattling questions fired at the Veda, in a manner most unlike her mother. Eventually she heard Clarine's voice relax, and the discussion end with an assurance that Nola would be strong enough to travel tomorrow.

She listened intently, trying to hear if the Veda would reveal how she had been in the room with Conri and yet unseen. But there was nothing to explain how, in the moments after Nola had fallen to the ground amid a desiccated Conri, it seemed to her that the Veda had stepped out from the dark mica walls. Later she had checked there was no door, she had not stepped from a secret room.

As she washed and changed her clothes, she overheard snatches of the Veda's exchange with the outside planets. She counted nine different voices in conversation with the Veda. Again, and again the speakers mentioned a crisis.

'Everything is at stake in this crisis...'

'The crisis is truly upon us...'

'I never thought I would live to witness the crisis...'

'It is good we have long prepared for the day of crisis.'

Now, in clean overalls, Nola sat opposite the Veda tracing her finger along a silver frame. The communicator, recessed into the table, formed a capable neural network of thinly layered nanites smeared on a clear sheet resembling the local devices that allowed Ailm's settlers to link together across the planet. The Veda's version linked planets together across the galaxy. Nola's finger tracked each shining corner hoping the Veda would talk to her about the 'crisis'. She felt compelled, already involved, but in what she did not know.

***

'Nola, it was a clever ploy to drape your manteau over the chair. You outwitted him. You're quick and certain in thought and action.'

The Veda's words roused Nola from her silence. She reached across the table and tenderly stopped Nola's hand incessantly outlining the silver rim on the table. Nola felt the strangeness of tears burning down her face: her breath quavered; her doleful sobs filled the room. The Veda stayed by her side, murmuring the softest sounds. Eventually, Nola lifted her head, bloodshot eyes searching the Veda's steady gaze. Her words stuttered like sharp barbs.

'I have killed, Veda. I killed another living thing - a thinking person.'

Drained beyond further anguish, Nola distilled her torment in that single thought The taking of a life, any life on Ailm was barely conceivable, a possibility merely acknowledged in myth and long-ago-stories. Realising she had broken the settlers most basic convention and despite her minds attempt to distract her she was traumatised.

'Accept what I say now, Nola. You had no choice but to act as you did. If Conri lived, then we did not. None of us on Ailm would exist after tomorrow.'

The Veda emphasised each word in her silken, precise manner. There was no trickery in her words.

'You acted for the greater good. You are absolved, though I know the weight of this experience will remain with us both all our days.'

The rich tones in the Veda's voice cocooned Nola in a reassuring aura, her sobs finally subsided. The Veda guided Nola to a cot in the corner of the cave. Resigned to her exhaustion, she lay down and slept.

***

Nola woke to the smell of breakfast cooking, aromas rising just like home. For a moment she thought she was in her own bed. In the firing of a neuron, though, she was overwhelmed by the rush of events. Somehow the dark cave was steeped in amber light, and when the Veda called her name, she could not pretend to be asleep.

'Nola, join me for breakfast and we can start this first day in a new era together. We have much to discuss.'

They ate and talked. Nola had decided in the early rush of memories, of guilt and shame and fear that she would tell the Veda everything, everything that had delivered her to the moment of ending Conri's life in the mica cave.

'Well, that is the whole story, Grand-mama. I put you in danger, put us all in danger because of my curiosity. Because I couldn't do exactly as Mama instructed me. You don't have to be kind to me. I understand I've failed the test.'

Nola finished her story gazing at the floor. The Veda sat in silence pondering Nola's words. After a few moments she spoke almost in a whisper.

'You have learnt many lessons in this short time. But be assured Conri's kind caused this. You did not place us in danger. He was not a traveller who happened upon hard times. He was the first in an advance party forced to crash land here because his technology failed. Do you understand? This was not your fault.'

'I think I understand, Grand-mama. If he hadn't been scouting the planet, he would not have crashed here. But why would anyone want to do that? Destroy us? We are peaceful people. The Quiet People.

'Conri and his friends will not bother us. At least not for now. His world, wherever it is, goes on without him. I'm sure you heard me speak with our cosmic neighbours. Our friends have aided us; they rallied to repel an advance mission. Our neighbours are more knowledgeable in matters of space travel, and Conri's craft has been recovered. He was indeed waiting on his friends. Your encounter was opportune.'

'But how can we know the intention of the mission? Perhaps they wanted to... they could be friendly... could they not?'

Nola shrugged her shoulders hearing the despair in her own question.

'On this matter, Nola, we can be confident. One of our neighbours, Luxii, on the outer edges of the spiral, already suffered an attack. Two days ago, they did not complete a check in link. The planet is devastated. Nothing survived. I did not exaggerate when I said you saved us all.'

Clasping her hands tightly in her lap, Nola drew in a sharp breath. Her voice pleading, her eyes again brimmed with tears, struggling to understand the scale of the catastrophe and for the first time feeling the quake of chaos around her.

'Everyone? A whole planet, people just like us? What can we do? Grand-mama, what happens now? Will others like Conri come here?'

'Somehow the balance in the universe is upset and his people are prepared to destroy worlds. Advancers noted throughout this galaxy are now in retreat. If this had not happened we – well, it isn't just Ailm saved today. The time is coming, Nola, for us to honour our alliances, to protect life here on Ailm, and across our galaxy. Life will change most for us few ready to step outside our world.'

The Veda nodded as she reached forward to catch Nola's tears before another fell.

'As for your mother, Clarine is proud you have passed the test against unknowable forces. Yes, Nola, before you ask, I said *passed*. Reflect on this, you can secure your place amongst the worlds for we have many battles ahead. The quiet time for some of us has passed. Indeed, your curiosity is a good thing. You still have a lot to learn, if, of course, you are willing.'

The Veda's wrinkled face look more earnest to Nola now. In the rich light, she reminded her of her mother as she would wait for Nola to settle her own mind. Nola felt a comfortable calmness, something she had not experienced for a long time. She accepted there were things she did not know, but in time she determined she would understand.

'Yes, Grand-mama, I do believe I am willing.'

The Veda smiled the smile of shared secrets, her grey eyes and red hair once again lighting the room.

'Nola, the way is not always straight or easy, for any of us who choose a different journey.'

There was both sadness and solace in the Veda's words. She leant forward and draped Nola in the warmth of her existence.

'Are you prepared to help protect our world, all the worlds?'

A hard determination rose from Nola's soul.

'Yes, Veda, I am ready. I feel it is time to step from the shadow.'

The Veda cupped her gnarled hands over Nola's.

'I think, my dear, you are quite right.'

Smoke Screens

When it comes to understanding human nature there's no one to beat me.

Louie smiled to himself as he edged through the hotel's quaint revolving door. Its brass polished to reflect the inflated expectation of arrivals and departures. He set his laptop bag in the boot and hung up his Saville Row jacket in the back of the Range Rover Sport. He stepped back to admire its clean lines, chuckling to himself, so far, he had managed to convince the car hire company to give him a free upgrade by claiming their incompetence had messed up his booking.

Works every time. He chuckled to himself.

Remembering too, the seeds he had already planted with the hotel receptionist, sharing a confidence about his 'hoards of online followers,' each one tracking his every move and hanging on his every word about his trip to Northern Ireland.

She was a cute little thing, her eagerness to please betrayed her daddy issues like a homing beacon. Her eyes had lingered just a few seconds too long on his Rolex watch.

Reading people in these hick places is almost too easy. No sophistication.

The sat nav primed and Bluetooth connected he set off on his journey. One hour ten minutes plus forty minutes for traffic and a coffee stop, he should be at his appointment in good time.

Even the roads are quaint here. So few motorways but they seem to manage.

He had already decided it was a strange country of elementals and extremes. He found it hard to put his finger on it but these people were tense on a subconscious level, matter of fact and welcoming externally, but deeply wounded. He shrugged the feeling off and imagined it slide down his shoulders and languish in the foot well.

'Only save the useful stuff. Unless it eases my way its just a throwaway.' He recited to the empty car.

Louie connected with his usual daily routine, first check in with his wife, Adele. She was her usual bleary morning self, but given two espressos and an hour she would be wrestling the day into shape, by the horns. He studied her voice, careful, not to alert her to his scrutiny. He related the funny set up at the airport and the upgrade to his rental. She finished with a yawned sentence.

'I've meetings back-to-back but ring me tonight. Best of luck today, my love.' And she was gone.

Next to business, he phoned his secretary, Danny. A few issues with the publisher were sorted easily and some promotional dates were set. With his fourth book due on the shelves soon TV interviews were mooted by the publisher keen to promote sales. Danny confirmed the media training was scheduled for his return to London next week. Before they ended the call Danny cleared his throat to indicate a change in topic.

'Oh, and Louie there's another message from 'Stephie won't leave my second name' ...checking I passed on her earlier messages. That's the lot. Mmmm... How is your hotel there?'

Danny gave himself a mental kick but he couldn't think of anything else to say. Stephie had phoned the office at least ten times and practically accused him of not doing his job.

The information was unwelcome for Louie too. The golden thread just unravelled a tad more in his mind and he needed to end the call.

'Yeh, yes, all good this end Danny. I'll check in later. Traffic is getting heavy here.' He lied, ending the call.

Ranking up the air con he chased the bead of sweat down his forehead. He tried to quell the 'oh shit' revolt in his brain, his dry-mouth thickened and his ragged breath felt tightened by the seat belt.

'Surely she got the message when I didn't ring back.' Again, the empty car failed to reply.

He recalled his instincts had screamed at him to walk out of that coffee bar. Stephie wasn't just out for fun but ... she was intriguing. Sitting alone, elegant hands turning the cup clockwise then anti-clockwise, the trace of perfume seeking him out, demanding his attention. Long dark hair and grey-blue eyes reeled him in. Why did beauty muddy the game? He never recognised a difficult read until it was too late.

'I need coffee and a break. I need to calm myself down.'

The Tim Horton's sign delivered another unwelcome flashback to his Canadian trip and the encounter with the infamous Stephie. Sitting in the car at the service station trembling fingers sought his pulse, it was racing. Sweat seemed to bubble on his forehead and he fished tissues from the glovebox. He stared at the fuel pumps to try to gather his thoughts. He felt soothed observing the drivers negotiating the most mundane of tasks. He imagined how they watched the numbers flash past, numbing the tension of life.

'Break it down into small bits Louie. You know how to deal with this. Getting coffee and a break to stretch my legs is a good idea and I've time to do that. No need to get into a panic here and now. Park this for later.'

Satisfied with his positive self-talk he strode out across the car park and caught the coffee machine in his cross-wires. But the smell of that coffee was determined to drag him to a place he did not want to be. He was overheating and the coffee cup felt like a branding iron in his fist. Standing in the queue to pay he picked up a packet of mints and as he reached the counter he heard himself say to the assistant,

'Yes, these thanks and I'll have a pack of cigarettes too, and a box of matches - doesn't matter what brand.'

Louie exited at a trot and flung himself around the back end of the Range Rover. His coffee rested on the roof, he clenched the cigarette packet as if he was about to lob an unringed grenade. The gross cover pictures screamed *danger, danger* at him.

Don't do it, just shake it off. You know you can.

He tossed the packet aside only to retrieve it as quickly, dusting off small fragments of gravel. He rescued the least bent smoke stick. With each moment the long abandoned ritual magnified its anticipated effect. He dragged the smoke into his lungs and belched it out on an industrial scale until it was barely a stub between his fingers.

Back in the car he used wipes like a murderer trying to rid himself of forensic evidence. He drank his cold coffee in one swallow. Louie put the mints on the passenger seat and set about eating them in twos and threes as he drove into the unfamiliar city. He avoided his own gaze in the mirror as he changed lanes, his knuckles bleached as he gripped the steering wheel.

She isn't going to stop phoning, that's clear. I'm going to have to speak to her, try to sort this out, somehow. Damage limitation required. Adele won't tolerate another dalliance.

Louie barely restrained himself from the urge to head bang the steering wheel. The air con worked in double time now and his journey slowed coming into city traffic. In a few minutes he was parked and striding into the venue. The floor manager greeted him warmly.

'Mr Swaye, great to see you again, I'm Jimmy, we met in London. I'll just get you miked up here and we will be ready for you after the introduction.'

'Ah, yes Jimmy good to see you. Let's get the show on the road then.'

On cue Louie breezed with practised confidence onto the stage, checking for his middle mark he swung round and raised his arms, white shirt sleeves rolled to his elbows, Rolex locked in the car. The lighting shielded him from the faces of a thousand people in his audience. Momentarily, he thought his falsehood was visible to all.

'Yes, thank you for that kind intro. I am indeed Louie Swaye and I'm here today to share with you my globally successful approach to stopping smoking … for good. Just take a moment folks to imagine that... you can stop smoking... forever.'

Louie turned side on to the multitude and walked across the stage nodding his head. Each look and gesture choreographed to compel their submission.

'My new book, 'Commit to Quit', will be on sale in the foyer after this event. But first let me tell you about my personal journey of discovery and how I quit smoking - for good.'

Trials of Kainos

Rowan shakes the night dust from his hair and rubs his beard rousing himself to the new day. Low-slung, the sun's pink tinged beams dissect the irregular horizon. The still air is cool, he sniffs and scans for anything unusual. He listens, every sense straining to refocus on the sounds around him. Striving to detect anything odd, anything that could harm him.

His thoughts merge into a vagueness that has made its home in his brain. Lingering dream images envelop his shallow awareness. A picture book, pulses primary colours. Smooth inviting pages dance onto his lap. His sisters small hand warm in his as they listened to a story. A soft blanket drapes his body and then her voice, whispers words of hope before dissolving into the mist. Stay safe and keep focused. Come back to me. Is that her again? Choking back the half-memory he abandons his urge to follow the speaker. He retraces the jumble in his mind, wrestling to separate his senses from the gloom. Drawing an uncertain conclusion he hoists the aged rucksack onto his back, its weight forcing air from his too-tired lungs. For now, he feels safe. Safe enough to continue.

His walk begins, alone with disconnected thoughts, alone with the world. He picks his strides carefully, not a forced march or a country stroll. He imposes no rhythm to his progression as he shadows the faint line of the once- upon-a-time road. Surrounded by disruption and decay the terrain tumbles like burst blisters conceding to ditches and craters. Over a few hours the sun follows his back and the terrain changes little until he crests the rim of a deep gouge. Smatterings of vegetation give way to a thick expanse of switch grass.

A vague sense of dread creeps along from the pit of his stomach along his vagus nerve. A derelict building with three archways and other jagged derelicts mitre the skyline sparking something in his memory. The stretching greenery and the stench of what once was reinforce a feeling of attachment. In an instant his heart rate increases and dry gasps constrict his throat dragging him back to the more pressing matter. His perpetual concern resurfaces.

'Am I safe, am I safe?'

And then he hears it, corrupting the silence, draining his hope. A steady crack, crack and the humming of something powered by - he can't remember what. That is a puzzle for later. Now he must hide before he is discovered. It would be the end of everything.

A quick survey of the terrain and he reckons the three archways will offer him the only hidey- hole he can reach before he starts. One final check for the disturbance, just to be sure. Then he is off, scrambling across moss wrapped masonry and thorny plants. He keeps his body as low to the ground as he can while striding out at top speed. Halting at intervals between debris heaps he reviews his progress. Listening, he checks the direction and frequency of the sounds, new dimensions added with each stop. His eyes dart the area feeding the route directly to his legs.

Reaching the arches, he does not stop, or look behind. Instead, he skips into the mouth of the middle arch. He slides the rucksack round to his front as he gulps the suddenly dank air. Closing his eyes in the darkness he slides down the wall resting on his hunkers. The dapple of the light dances on his retina as he tries to quiet his breathing and slow his booming heart. Surging blood pulses against his eardrums dampening his hearing.

It's there again. The noise. Different now as it draws closer. The sound more nuanced, mimicking the rhythm of his beating heart. Clutching the bag closer to his chest he tries to become the shadow and melt into the wall.

Seconds feel like minutes, time stretching every nerve in his body. He dares to move again but not towards the daylight. Rowan's hand stretches out feeling the wall. He is surprised by the smooth surface. Standing now he inches into the depth of the archway. Seeking some security in the darkness he gropes further into the gaping tunnel. The noise is getting closer. He can feel vibrations coursing through his veins. He freezes, rooted to the ground. The Watcher hovers, limbs billowing, an erratic silhouette framed by the archway. He binds the bag closer to his chest muffling his racing heartbeat from the Watcher's sensors. And then he closes his eyes to wait, silent trembles wrack his body. He has never been this close to a Watcher before, never wanted to be this close.

Old encounters with the Watchers' claw for his attention. Unsure if the memories are real or imagined. Craving some tenfril of clarity he sifts through his panic. Nothing connects. Nothing makes any sense to him. All he can do is stay still and quiet. The Watcher is in the archway now. In the darkness the evil red eyes spin, churning the atmosphere creating waves that make

Rowan believe every cell in his body is about to burst. He is statue-still, too fearful to draw a breath. Beads of sweat team down his face, his mouth has never felt so dry and every joint in his body locks rigid.

The Watcher is closer now. He is almost at his limit craving another breath. He raises his thoughts above his terror in these final moments, praying for a better life the next time. Resigned to his fate as the Watcher draws almost parallel with his position his hand finds a chink in the surface. As he struggles between breathing and passing out the wall gives way behind him and he rolls into a space.

The force of hitting the ground presses air into his starving lungs. Rowan gasps what he thinks will be his last breath. The light is so bright he thrusts his arm over his face shielding his eyes from pain. Everything is white hot searing as his body struggles to define this new place. The smells, the sounds, the touch are all unnerving and yet familiar. His question rises to the surface.

'Am I safe?'

Realising he has spoken aloud he is astonished to hear his name.

'Rowan, you are safe'.

He wants to believe the speaker, he wants to be safe and yet something nips at the edges of his mind.

***

In the stark cramped space Cepta kneels cradling the fetal Rowan. Her hands cup the sides of his face shielding him from the sudden light. She makes soft reassuring sounds just as their mother did when they were children.

To steady his agitation, she looks directly into his eyes. She studies his face. At one time more familiar to her than her own, now grey and bearded. Searching for soft brown eyes she knows so well, now wild with fear and his body, once solid and powerful, withered to skin and bone. Her eyes plead for a sign he is still there, that Rowan her brother hasn't forgotten her and their life, their plans. The urge to wrap her arms around him and weep for everything they have lost is quelled by their community's strict protocols. This protocol governing returnees was drilled into every Drumlyn citizen.

Seconds tick away before they are joined by the others and Rowan is launched into the depth of the facility. She is struck by a vivid memory. Her small hand secure in Rowan's as they walked together for the first time to the doctrine group. Rowan soothing the inside of her wrist to ease her nerves. She stretched her legs just that little more to match him step for step. When he realised her small struggle, he shortened his step to suit her better And the smile, the most wonderful Rowan smile, made it all seem normal.

Taking inspiration from her memory she lets her mind click into the list of standard tasks. Cepta usually found solace in the predictability of the doctrine, now it feels cold and brittle as she raises them both to their feet. Holding him steady she worries he could float away without her as his anchor. In the quiet moment before the others arrive she allows herself to offer him reassurance, whispering in his ear.

'Rowan, stay focused, you're home now. Relax, there are no Watchers here.'

In her mind she curses the Harmony Doctrine governing every aspect of life. An image of the Prime group and their number one, Kopp deepens her fear, her loathing. An often-observed scene rears up pressing cold fingers along her spine. six figures sit in the Perusal room, shoulders stooping over consoles, faces grim in blue screen light, fingers arched and lips pursed in concentration They scroll and scoop and scrutinise every aspect of the continuous record of every moment for every person in Drumlyn. Even now, this moment and those to follow are prescribed and recorded to be dissected and analysed by the Primes.

She stands with her back to the opaque wall, behind the divider the remainder of Rowan's set waits. Four figures stand ready for the signal to enter. Bile rises stinging her throat as she releases the divider. Aware this reaction too is instantly committed to the record. And so, it is with Rowan upright, his eyes locked on her as if his life depends on that connection, the next stage begins.

The others pause for a microsecond before stepping into action. Cepta instinctively holds him until the last moment, determined to protect him from this new assault on his senses. The four move in swiftly releasing Rowan from her arms. They act with one mind, with one purpose and without one word. She continues to hold his hand, as they gently lower him onto a gleaming gurney. Simultaneously the first regime of drugs are injected. He succumbs to the sedation, his hand relaxes. Finally, he blinks and closes his eyes. The room descends underground.

***

Later, nearing the end of evening rota, Cepta visits Rowan in the returnee suite of the Medical Unit. Stepping into the dim, warm room her fears resurface with renewed energy. Pings and beeps punctuate the silence. Rowan's set is still on duty and Jet, their medic, greets her.

'Quite a day Cepta. Good to see you. I just need to complete this set of observations and administer the next batch of medications. It will take me about fifteen minutes. Then I can give you a better update. If you prefer to wait have a seat.'

'Jet, yes, a great day to have Rowan return to us from the surface. Forgive my late interruption. This is the first opportunity I have had to come over. I'll let you complete your work while I wait.'

She swivels the spare stool and sits down, hands resting in her lap, she watches Jet survey the array of instruments attached to Rowan. Noting, ticking adjusting with practised efficiency just like everything that happens in Drumlyn. She scrutinises every aspect of the room, the bed, except Rowan's bed, afraid she will want to rush to hold her brother's hand or bury her tears in his chest. Triggers and memories have haunted her all day, leaking from the previously well concealed vault. Things she had not thought about in many years dribbled and sprung into her conscious mind.

The first time she met Jet they sat beside each other at their introductory session to Harmony Doctrine. For that first lesson they gathered in the congress room. Twelve seven and eight year old children sat swallowed in the belly of a huge oval arena. Tiers of seating faced onto a central platform. She remembered that was the first time they wore grey and green coveralls like their parents. The roughness of the material had made her fidget, so mother made sure in the weeks leading up to that day the coveralls were softer and Cepta was acclimatised. Mother was stricter than father in many ways, but softer too. Sitting with one child either side, her arms encircled their shoulders as they nestled into her. Dark curls brushed her narrow shoulders and her pale oval face held their attention every time as she told their story, their history.

That day in the congress room Cepta sat still, just like all the other children. The Prime was a tall man, lean and dark in his black coveralls. His steps echoed around the room as he paced up and down, hands linked behind his back, his head straining in front of him. A clipped sharp tone matched his angular features and kept them all alert. Their faces mirrored his impassivity.

'Children, you have all come to an age now where your investment in Drumlyn begins. As a cloistered community managing every aspect of life, from food and energy production to community compliance, is critical to our survival.'

He scanned each young face as he spoke pausing to ensure he had their attention.

'Of course, that includes population size. It is a cornerstone of our effectiveness, of our success. The family extension lottery runs twice every ten years. Sometimes the barren period needs to be longer. At this point in your young lives you need not concern yourselves with that. What in means is, in our community, age distribution clusters into neat little groups. Just perfect for all the training you will need to form your new sets and continue to uphold our way of life.'

Cepta wanted to ask questions but Rowan caught her eye, a reminder she must not ask anything outside their own home. It was a house rule.

'Here, in this group, there will be two sets. Your tutors will make the division and allocate designation in five years. Each set as you know requires specific roles. Your parents all have a purpose. From planners to primes, six is the optimum number. Each set has the capacity to operate independently should the need arise. You will soon understand this is just one of the pillars of our society, designed to ensure a future for humanity.'

The Prime ended his session with a long and ardent statement reminding them how privileged they were to be alive and living in Drumlyn 14.

'Remember children, Life is Loyalty, Harmony is Essential. It all starts here.'

The sounds reverberated long after his words had finished.

Memories of her mother threaten tears, they always do. Preparing her for the strictures of Drumlyn, as well as the families own mission, had been much more difficult than with Rowan. Formal lessons were supplemented by their mother and father. After their evening meal, the unique little set remained at the table, dishes pushed aside, the real learning would pick up where the last ended or sometimes some occurrence would prompt a different line of discussion. Their family quest, the Kainos mission, handed down through innumerable generations formed the bedrock of their dual existence. Everything revolved around external conformity and internal secrecy.

She is glad neither of her parents are here to see this, see Rowan return like a ghost from the crust. She swallows back the grief, reburying past pain, just as her parents had taught her. Her father's soft voice reached out with words of consolation.

Remember Cepta outside of home you must be focused, show no emotion. Ask only permitted questions. You have your game face so use it. Never let it slip. Life depends on us, on our mission. This here in Drumlyn, it's a small inconvenience, one we shall manage to overcome.

She pictures his soft brown eyes, the scrape of his beard and warm breath as he tucks covers around her each bedtime. The time they sorted and sifted the events of the day, a way to manage her alter self. The shape of his broad shoulders, signified dependability, and love to her. She felt safe in his shade. Panic and pain were soothed and exuberance rechannelled and curtail. He could offer her reassurance or advise restraint across a room, just like Rowan.

Jet completes his assessment and waves Cepta over to the bedside. He honours her with eye contact, a softening in his features. He almost smiles. She responds with a slight incline of her head in acceptance. Both know, if questioned by the record, they can justify their response to each other. Cepta accepts the stool offered by Jet beside Rowan's bed.

'I have just entered the report to Prime set so I can share his position with you as his blood relation.'

'That would be good. Jet thank you. He is looking better than he did earlier.'

'It's a standard returnee pathway with additional boosters to offset the length of his exposure. His figures are coming up quite well, physically. Though I'd like to see them higher. We are replacing and filtering blood, repopulating enzymes, trace elements and natural bacterium. Decontamination is complete. Quarantine will last another 40 hours. It's precautionary, to rule out anything else. Rowan has had boosters for accelerated muscle restoration and weight gain. So, in a few days his strength will begin to improve. It's a slow process as you know. And earlier I forwarded his clothes and pack to Prime upon their request.'

Drawing a short breath Cepta decides to ask the question she has been dreading.

'That all sounds reasonably positive... at least physically. What about his mind, his memories? Do you know yet if they will return?'

Jet pauses to consider his answer. Aware of the continuous record he chooses his words carefully.

'Well, the level of exposure Rowan has endured is considerably more than we have encountered to date. I've administered synaptic enhancers and neuron builders to help. Once he is conscious, though, stimulation and orientation will play a key role in the level of recovery. Rowan is not alone in this. He has the support of his set and you, as his sister and his second, you will be critical in his rehabilitation.'

Jet rubs his forefinger along his eyebrows and glances at her, a glance that says he has said all he can for now.

He turns his attention to the bank of monitors. Making minor adjustments he focuses on the readouts, resisting any urge to offer more hope, more consolation than the doctrine permits. Cepta knows while there is a degree of latitude Jet must feel close to that limit.

Every nerve in her body strains, urging her to resist asking more questions. She wants to know if Rowan said anything? Did it seem like he knew where he was? What was the chance of him being her brother again? Had Jet noticed anything about his clothes when he was undressing him or in his pack? Who in the Prime set made the request for his belongings? How has he survived ninety-seven days above ground? Any one of those would surely put them both under special scrutiny, something to be avoided at all costs, especially now. Instead, she turns toward Rowan. Without his beard his face is gaunt, thin lips drawn tight against his teeth, in an eerie half-grin. He is frozen in a deep drugged sleep. Cepta realises she must freeze this turmoil in her head.

'I understand Jet, thank you, for everything. May I stay, sit with him for a while. Just until the end of this duty period?'

'Yes Cepta. I'm sure Rowan would benefit from that. I'm just over there if anything is needed and then we can join the others in quarantine.'

The cacophony from medical equipment and the almost imperceptible rise and fall of his chest are the only signs to tell her Rowan is alive. She moves her stool a little closer. She feels Jet move away and step over to his bank of monitors. It never ceases to amaze her how so much could be said with so few words.

***

After a few hours with Rowan, she leaves for the quarantine suite. Their direct contact with Rowan on his return requires decontamination and time in isolation. As she walks along with Jet they rehearse the rehabilitation plan they will discuss with the others. With every fibre in her body, she yearns to return home, the only place in Drumlyn there is any privacy for people. The only place to be yourself. To think clearly. Cepta hopes Jet doesn't notice her racing heart, her shallow breath as she struggles to focus on the quest. Maintaining this facade, this secret life consumes her. The hands of fate tighten around her throat. Mental exhaustion, confusion and fear erodes her fortitude as they near the isolation room. With no legitimate reason to ask for Rowan's backpack her only way to find out what has happened is through Rowan. She has no idea if their quest is any nearer it's end, only Rowan knows.

Jet has already provided his update on Rowan's well-being so there would be little they could add and few questions to field. Sipan, Begley and Loxton greet them at the door of the isolation room. Despite grey faces, tired stances and the ever-present record there is a warm buzz in the room. For the first time since Rowan's departure Cepta feels their closeness. They have food waiting, not a feast, or a celebration just welcome sustenance. Sitting together, they eat quietly. They only ask her two questions. How are you? And what is the plan to help Rowan? That is all they ask of her.

Later, lying on a narrow cot surrounded by the steady breathing of her set, Cepta is again amazed by how so few words communicate so much.

Waves of memory wash on the beach of her exhausted psyche. The background to Rowan's mission percolates through the levels of her mind. Concern was triggered when Drumorhis 11 failed to reply to their regular verification call. Drumorhis' radio had been unreliable for many years and they had no more spare parts. In the way of the Drums this possibility was ranked, considered and a response agreed between the Drums in advance. So once the check-in was missed the plan was activated. Rowan volunteered to deliver the replacement radio. It should have taken no more than fourteen days. Cepta recalls his inscrutable acceptance of the mission when he spoke with Kopp and his excitement once they were alone at home. This excursion would provide the first opportunity to this generation of the Kainos family to search for another section of the solution. He was sure this was the opportunity they needed, what they trained to do. How the solution would help those living in the Drums they didn't know but every member of the Kainos family was committed to the quest.

As Rowan packed and plotted his trek no one mentioned the significance of losing contact with the only other remaining Drum. No one mentioned the dangers of going above ground for even a short period of time. No one mentioned the implications of their silence. Or the thundering silence of the other one hundred and nine Drums that just dropped out of existence since Drum history began. Underground communities, Drums, were created to preserve humanity. Now Drumlyn 14 seems to be very much alone. Rowan had left ninety-seven days ago. Contact with Drumorhis hasn't resumed. Retracing events, calmly ordering her thoughts, helps reminds her she is the planner, and she is Kainos, so she can do whatever it takes. Then she sleeps, dreaming of all the Cepta's and Rowan's who have gone before them all, dedicated to the Kainos quest. Each generation confident they will contribute line by line to the solution.

Noise and urgency and light burst into Cepta's sleep. Shot into a consciousness she isn't yet ready to feel, a day she isn't prepared to face. Numbered by the attraction of oblivion she struggles to open her eyes, struggles to connect to the voice shouting at her from the doorway. Then she hears if clearly.

'Quick Cepta come now. He's awake, he's asking for you.'

#Neurasthenia

Tyler had pulled an all-nighter, again. In fact, he had been playing continuously for over forty-three hours. He thought there should be some sense of triumph as he was the last man standing. He had invested hundreds of hours and lost many friends working steadily up the rankings, to this point.

One point eight million viewers watched him dispatch his friend Stig in the final level to win the competition. Before he sat down to play he had savoured the thrum of endorphins flooding his veins and arteries. He felt invincible. Now, winning had never felt so hollow. There was no urge to fist pump the air or utter gloating consolations. He didn't even want to watch the congratulations roll on screen or take note of his cash pot immediately lodged in his bank account. Anti-climax had hit him this time in an instant. The pixelated cover was snatched off his pit of anguish again and the longing to be back online screamed his name.

The detritus of his stint fringed his elite gaming chair. Water bottles emptied and refilled with gradually darkening urine lined one side of his position. On the other Red Bull cans lay crushed, disguarded like the bodies left behind in the game. A haphazard cliff of moving crates in one corner entombed his long-forgotten family photos and life's essentials.

Instinctively he eased the headset off. The heat in the room was stifling, humidity-loaded, a combination of his sweat and the struggling coolers on the PC. The curtains were closed, he had no clue if it was day or night. He thought it didn't really matter, he hadn't been outside in, well, he didn't really remember the last time. His brain refused to do the calculation. A memory of rain, an impromptu shower releasing the hope of a new-born spring pushed for attention. He found it a painful thought to follow. Too painful. His brain felt a cascade of cauterising explosions, as if it had subsumed the hundreds of devices triggered during the tournament and was releasing them in a rattle of retribution.

Tilting back into the headrest he rocked his head from side to side. He pressed his hands over his ears to try to block the sound. Reflex snapped his palms away. The rising heat almost seared his hands. He just couldn't avoid the high frequency buzzing in his ears, it seemed to oscillate, lapping around his brain. As the sound intensified the temperature rose, allied for no logical reason. He imagined he felt his fillings rattling like an aftershock from some unknown event. His heart fibrillation amplified around his body, racing a micro current at laser speed. Flashing after-images filled his entire field of vision even as he closed his eyes. He tried to move his legs, there was no response. He tried his arms, they had moved just a moment ago. No response.

Bile rose from his belly, he vomited. Not an involuntary response, head thrusting forward to keep the airways clear. Paralysis prevented that, his lungs frothed and spurted as he choked bucking out of his chair. Realising what was happening his body tried. But tried too late.

The red power light blinked in a kind of sadness but not really sad...more disappointed. Red had seen this before. Tyler's circuitry had overheated, combusted and finally burned out. Irretrievable. Red knew the backdoor into Tyler's tasty neurosis, through the game, was useless, no neurons firing meant no feast. A message relayed to other kin let them know they were moving on. Time to find another Tyler. After years spent with him, Red didn't blink twice, leaving the router far behind to join the mainframe in search of another long term project.

Hidden in Plain Sight

Erin lifted the mail from the sand-trap mat. Two brown envelopes.

'Bill and bill,' she tossed them on the hall table.

The third was not a bill. It was handwritten, a flourish of loops on a stiff white envelope. Her name, *Erin Littlewood,* sheepishly waited for her to notice it. Turning the envelope over and back she watched tiny lights dance across the pearlized surface. Flicking the back of the envelope she recalled seven cards last Christmas and four text messages on her birthday. Her circle of contacts had admittedly diminished. She bit her lip focusing her powers of deduction on the card, pivoting it between her fingers. It refused to give away any secrets. The script was unfamiliar and she could not think of any significant events coming up. The only thing to do if she wanted to know who had sent it and what it was about was open the card. She tapped the envelope against her lower lip. With a decisive twist of her wrist, she propped it on the table.

'Later' she nodded at the white wrapped puzzle.

Picking up Raggles' lead was like the first tap of a conductor's baton. He was ready to play, his excitement bubbled, nearing chaos. Twice daily with the turn of the tide they trekked along the beach. Tide out, coat on, her rescue collie tugging eager on his well-stretched lead.

'If we delay another second, you will surely combust. Can't have that now, can we? Come on, good boy.'

He calmed just enough for her to clip the lead onto his collar. As ever the thunk of the closing door echoed, intense and hollow, incongruous in her small bungalow. No matter how abundant her soft furnishings and deep pile rugs, the sound of desolation was deep-rooted, inescapable. Its sonic imprint lingered. This stinging reminder filled a place he had never lived. The walls had never chimed with his deep tones, his *enjoy your walk* chuckle had never rippled these walls.

***

Close readings of police reports and visits to the accident site had only intensified her confusion. She felt simultaneously mired in despair and dislocated from her own psyche. Without him she existed, just existed. She knew he would never have wanted to leave her, not like this. Frozen in shock, suspended between a world she refused to accept and a world she could never restore, she sought answers in floating feathers and fence-hopping Robins. Searching his pockets and flipping through the pages of his books for some sign, some note, some secret message from him became a regular obsession. TV channels and radio stations were changed to map his habits, surely, he was reaching out – his favourite programme or piece of music could be significant.

'I just need to know where to look. Please, please... help me find a sign you are with me... Please.'

Invariably she found herself sitting in the midst of mayhem trying to create order, an order that
she could accept. Each evening she watched shadows grow in the darkness of their bedroom. It felt like trying

to interpret long ago cast runes or read faceless tarot cards.

***

Erin returned to work urged by relatives who hoped that routine would help her breathe a bit easier. Her colleagues in biostatistics welcomed her back. After all, she was the Research Lead with years of experience. She had mentored most of the team. Everyone was shocked when they saw her. Myrtle on reception, the weathervane of the team, reflected their concerns in the tea room.

'She just isn't herself, how could you expect her to be? She's obviously not eating, she's skin and bone. Not sleeping either I'd say. She won't let herself grieve- pure shock I'm sure.'

Something vital had changed in Erin. She pursued patterns that could not possibly exist either in the data or in life. Sifting for correlations that fell outside research, beyond the bounds of science. By the end of the third week she found herself still in her pyjamas scrutinising the texture on her breakfast toast at three o'clock one Friday afternoon. It was then she acknowledged that the sharp edge of the mental axe had separated her from her understanding of the world. Conrad's words returned to her time and again.

You, my darling can solve anything, you are my Solutionist.

She decided to retire.

***

After the second anniversary she recognised that her grief had exhausted family and friends. Those once supportive visits dwindled in frequency. Life in the city screamed infinite reminders of the cosmic shift, suffocating her. She imagined how concerns transmuted into relief when she decided to move nearer the sea. A seeker only seeking confirmation, or at least reassurance. Of what though, she really was not sure. Meaning and purpose and connectedness had left like morning mist carried on a last breath. On his last breath.

Looking back, Erin understood that the search had started after Conrad died, after the police had knocked the door, after his ashes were handed to her, after sympathies and explanations caught her in a web of inertia.

The first summer in the bungalow she had walked her stretch of beach in sandals. Curving along the dampened sand line, the granulated pulp squeezing between tanned toes bound in blue straps. The rasp of wet grains reminding her about touch. Ozone forced her to breathe, forced her to remember, charging her with energy she didn't want. The shifting character of the shore and dunes, sky and sea, a constant message - everything changes. Change she rejected.

Each time she tried to retrace her exact steps her path had been subsumed by nature's vigour. Pressing each foot precisely on the sand, right foot forward heel to toe, shifting her weight from her left sandal to the right, then repeat. Her imprint reclaimed each time. Like a ghost walking through this new life. Each outing in her sandals reminded her of Balos in Crete, their last holiday. There they had matched each other's stride for stride, hand in hand, too absorbed to notice their footprints didn't last there either. Perhaps there it didn't matter.

***

Now summer was a few turned pages on her calendar and autumn was succumbing to winter. As she strode out, her stout boots left a fading impression along the beach. The daily analysis continued with each morning walk. Clouds and contrails were scrutinised and dismissed, the froth of receding tide and the tangle of seaweeds were all given due consideration. She couldn't contemplate missing a sign, a signal, blinking at the wrong moment could be disastrous. The search for meaning permeated every aspect of her life.

Raggles' barking wrenched her back from her impromptu reverie. Her focus had wavered and she never wavered. She retrieved a whipping strand of brown hair and pushed it under her woolly hat. Raggles ran round her in semicircles herding her, his tail low, his eyes intent on bending her to his will. Erin moved obediently, curious to see what this display was all about.

He came to rest near the dunes, a paw either side a half-buried shell.

'Well boy, what have you found here? What is so important?

Erin bent down to ruffle his fur, usually a game changer for him. Not this time though, he continued to nose the shell, quite unlike a collie, unlike Raggles.

Without thinking she hunkered down to lever the shell from the wind-dried sand.

Bigger than it seemed, about the size of the palm of her hand. No razored edges or fatal flaws. She turned it over and back. It was the cup side of a scallop shell. Shaded ridges fanned out from the fractured hinge moving from earthy tones to flecks of flamingo pink. Inside it was smooth, fringed with grey and a perfect iridescent white begging to be touched. Cold finger tips traced along the stria. Only half of what it once was, yet still whole, still complete.

Raggles waited with unusual patience as she manoeuvred the shell through every angle. No one else witnessed it, but as Erin raised her eyes to the far horizon she knew she had found her lens. The long-clouded perspective dispersed. Not by a message, but something far simpler. A random element in all the hunted signs finally triggered her acceptance of her grief. Her solution. There was no missed pattern, no moment she had overlooked.

Like the half-buried shell, she was still whole. Conrad existed in her, in her memories, in each heartbeat and always would. She wiped her tears, her first tears from her pale blue eyes since Conrad died. Knocking the last few grains of sand from the shell she tucked it into her pocket. Turning into the wind they headed for home. Each step gaining renewed purpose. Her tears were there now, her grief was surfacing. The white envelope would be opened, the invitation accepted and she would make some long overdue calls. The scourge of the impossible search was relegated to the past.

I Am Here

Dedication In Memory
of
Sylvia Fleming

I Am Here

He runs, pounding the road. Long strides hammering through his bones and muscles. The distraction soothes him, he embraces the pain. Sweat saturates his body, tracing rivulets in the chill night. His backpack chafes his bony shoulders.

There was a time mastering his running technique was his only goal, always telling us about his training, timings, nutrition, distance, as we sat in Andrew's house. Then Andrew would tell us about how the world should be, how we must be, most importantly how we would help his mission. Colin struggled the most with the concept of 'Andrew's Way', the rest of us followers were more compliant. Hook, line and sinker, that's what Andrew called his method.

Now Colin just runs and runs. I've been with him almost every night these past four weeks, same route, same time, same memory. Dim moonlight tinting the contrail, tracing his route along the back road to nowhere.

At the beginning I visited different people, trying to connect. I've visited my Mum again today. Sat on her bed, the room in disarray. Mum was never the tidiest person but even this was extreme. Photos chequered the quilt, she lay fetal in the middle. Blood cried eyes stared into nothingness. A bottle of red wine collapsed on the floor. I've never known her drink, or cry, until now.

On *Day One,* thrashing in the confusion of my plight, I sought solace watching her sleep. She grew restless as I spoke to her, so I stopped. As the sun crept through the blinds we both ran to check if I had come home. Empty bed. She tried my mobile phone. It rang to voicemail.

' Bria this is Mum. Phone me as soon as you get this message... Its urgent.'

I paced the rooms with her as she rang work, friends, family. Each conversation similar, no one had seen or heard from me but they were sure I would turn up. Then utterly failing to quell her growing panic she phoned Casey, my sister. I listened as she calmed Mum down, she was always so good at that.

'Mum you need to ring Andrew, that's most likely where she spent last night. You've probably put yourself through all this for nothing.'

'God... yes I never thought. I'll ring now. God please let her be there... I'll be back to you.'

I thought my heart would break again as she pulled the post-it from the fridge door. When I told her we were serious I gave her his number but it never made it to her phone.

' Oh... Hi Andrew, Bria's mum here. Could I have a word with her?'

She held her breath, swaying back and forth as she watched the old swing frame in the garden. I could feel the swim of possibilities for her, promising herself she wouldn't be cross when I would come on the phone.

'Bria ... she isn't here. Last night she said she needed to go home to you. Things to sort out she said. Left here about eleven. Is there a problem?'

Listening to his voice now, so soft, intense, you could almost believe he cared.

'Oh... I'm... not really sure. She didn't come home last night and she hasn't turned up for work.'

'Goodness, I hope nothing has happened. I gather you guys had a bit of a tiff. I tried to calm her down. You know Bria though, that temper.'

The edge of amusement in his voice was obvious to a trained ear, his little game of cat and mouse would roll on. Mum finished off the call quickly as goosebumps chilled her arms. I stood by her elbow telling her, *don't believe a word he says, he knows where I am.*

Casey had checked the hospital just in case I had been involved in an accident and she was all over my social media pages when Mum phoned her back. No imprint of me, anywhere.

'I'm on my way home Mum I'll be with you in a couple of hours. Let me know if she turns up.'

Mum could barely speak. I tried to hug her, hardly a common gesture between us but a genuine reflex, an act of love.

We had rowed about Andrew, about how I was living my life. Disappointment had oozed from every pore, her face lobster red when I told her to butt out. Like a psychedelic reflection I can see the mask of my snugness as I fired my parting shots.

'Just 'cause you made an arse of your life doesn't mean I'll do the same.'

'It's a cult. For God sake Bria the man thinks he's the second-coming. I forbid you to see him. This stops now.'

I watch as I lowered my eyes. Like an old movie on slow shutter speed, I saw the exact moment. I just wanted to win. She handed it to me.

'Yes Mum... you're right. It stops now.'

How cruel I was as I let her think I was conceding. In

that moment she didn't realise the sword was in until I twisted it. And I didn't realise I twisted it for both of us.

'If you can't accept me, accept my choices... then we're finished. You'll never see me again.'

I spat the words and tore out of the house. That was the last time we saw each other.

***

I have visited her many times since. On *Day Two* in our living room I screamed, pleading for her to hear me, to help me, somehow.

She spoke with the officers giving my details, so many details, I never thought mum knew so much about me. Often, she seemed indifferent to me and my adventures. She was honest enough, she said I was involved with a group led by a man she didn't approve of and that we argued. That is true, she didn't tell them I told her she would never see me again. I guess at that time she didn't believe my threat was real or she was wise enough not to hand the police a credible line to completely discount my missing status.

Later though, I could see our argument haunt her, lashing her very spirit. I'm not sure mum is receptive but I pray something of what I say takes seed. Repeating words of forgiveness, begging her to keep looking for me.

I followed the officers to their car. A blatant announcement of trouble in our well-preserved cul-de-sac. The young woman, straight backed and stripped of make-up looked younger than me. Her dark hair stretched back like a prima ballerina. She was fine framed like me but much taller than my five foot two inches.

'I've got the heebie-jeebies. I think something bad has happened.' she said to her older male colleague. Shivers visible across her body. That was the first time I noticed that effect but not the last.

'When you've seen as many missing teenagers as I have you get a nose for it. She's either run off with this fella' or she'll be back in a couple of days with her tail between her legs and a great story for her social media pals.'

'OK, but we still look don't we Don?'

'Talk to her sister, family, friends, work colleagues. Check her bank cards for use, her phone, basically everything we got from her mum. The electronic picture goes on the database and out to all officers, ports and airports. Her disappearance will be covered at briefings too. So yes... we still look.'

'What about the group she is involved with? I think we start with them.'

'Yes, Kirsty, we'll get round to that... soon.'

Once a fine footballer, Don remained trim if not entirely fit. His short hair spiked wilfully around the band of his US style cap. Dark shadowed eyes had witnessed too many human hardships and horrors. I could see the knot of worry trapped between his shoulders as they opened the car. In that moment of quiet I jumped around Kirsty shouting right into her face. I saw her colour drain. Could she hear me?

'God Don I feel awful... hope I'm not coming down with that bug going round the station. Get the heat on for me please.'

Seems not, seems I could make people feel uneasy,

even ill but was that it?

***

My sister Casey is so different from Mum. Three years older than me, I envy how deftly she escaped mum's expectations. She was always focused on school, on career and then on Dylan. The first two I understood but to me Dylan was old before his time. They met on her study year abroad. I teased them about how she snuck him through customs as hand luggage. The joke being he was six foot seven and the luminescence factor dropped considerably when he stood in a doorway. The more I saw them together the less I understood what she saw in him. Casey finished her Business degree, got married, moved into their apartment and started her new job all within three months. A seamless string of major life events without any fuss or fluster.

I see now she is like a swan so elegant on the surface but underneath there is a lot happening. And Dylan, he isn't the drab man I judged him to be. In my curious state I've witnessed tiny acts of tenderness and support. He is her lightning rod protecting her. He quietly follows leads, using the media to keep my story on peoples' lips, in peoples' hearts. Everyone is looking for me, which would be great if I were missing, but I am here.

From *Day Two* Casey refused to believe I had just left, run out on my life without a word. She knew I had a hot temper but it never lasted long. I was there the first time she went to Andrew's house on *Day 8*. He perched on the broad arm of his leather sofa, the smell of bleach almost peeling the paint of the walls. Everything in its place, colour coded books, not a smidgen of dust, a bathroom where a forensic scientist would struggle to find a cell to prove I had ever been there. I know, *Day One* I had watched him scrub, scour, soak, steep, bleach, burn and dispose. Why don't they see the devil he is? I sit on his bed many nights while he sleeps the sleep of the righteous. I tell him what I think of him. I damn him for what he has done to me. He never stirs. My anger like fear ebbed away too.

'Well Casey, wasn't the turnout of volunteers great today. Hard to maintain though I'm sure without official sanction. I was up at forest park offering my support. People are so … kind. In a strange way I feel a bit responsible for her leaving town. How are you all keeping up?'

'Awh … Andrew it's just looking worse every day. Mum's falling apart. I don't know how much longer she can cope. The police say Bria's phone can't be traced, could be the battery is flat. Her bank cards haven't been used either. She's hasn't been in touch with anyone. No sightings either. You know as well as me that's not typical Bria, is it?'

She assumes an attitude of confusion and a lone tear rolls down her cheek. If it wasn't so serious and I wasn't worried about her safety I would laugh at the absurdity.

'It's not... but then what is typical behaviour changes over time and as circumstances shift. You getting married and moving away had a profound effect on her. She often told me how she resented being saddled with your mum. How she wanted to escape. Did she not speak to you about this? I suggested she should. Perhaps you were …

busy.'

As he speaks, he chases invisible fluff from his jeans and examines his nails before raising his hooded eyes to meet Casey's. Sharp memories jolt through me. I will Casey not to take the bait. I see now how he undermined everything I said and did, even what I thought. This was my life with him, feeling worthless and unworthy, needing to escape. After my argument with mum, I did rethink everything he was asking me to sacrifice. It was too much. Mum was right. Giving up my family, my friends, my career, I had given up so much already. I decided to tell him I was finished with the group and with him.

'Sure, you know how families are, up and down. She talks about you ...a lot though. You are very important to her. She must have been devastated when you ended things. I can only imagine how upset she was that night. How did she take it?'

Casey sat on the chair I usually occupied, head tilted, brown eyes and hair just like me. She was the epitome of concern, focused on Andrew yet she scanned the room, senses on high alert.

'Oh, you know Bria - lots of drama and tears.'

'Did it happen here?

'What?' For the first time he seemed uncertain.

'When you finished with her.'

'Mm mm... She was very immature, needy... I'm ashamed I let things go too far. The flesh is weak. Getting involved with a member of my flock, small as it is, shouldn't have happened. Look I really need to get ready for them now. We have a prayer circle... for Bria.'

He patted a bible sitting beside him and stood to guide her toward the door. I screeched for him to take his hands off my sister. I pleaded with her to just leave now while she had the chance.

That 'she was' swung it for Casey, that and my perpetual whispering in her sleeping ear at night. I did a lot of that. Casey, Mum, Andrew and Colin, of course.

Casey didn't mention to him the eye-watering bleach fumes or ask had he been doing a spot of cleaning but she was damned convincing when she recounted it all to the police two hours later. That did seem to be a turning point.

That night Dylan held her tight as deep sobs wrecked her body. The time with Andrew had exhausted her. He could syphon off your energy, his words like physical assaults.

'He has done something to her – past tense... he spoke about her as if she were dead...he has … I don't know ...has he killed her?'

They passed many nights like that but each morning they both faced the search again.

***

He was plausible, that was the word the officer used when he updated Mum, Casey and Dylan on *Day 13*. Andrew told the police it was unfortunate I didn't get along with my mum and I often talked about leaving to make my fortune in London or Paris. Emphasising how headstrong I was, a dreamer who freaked out when he ended our relationship. I was too intense. In fact, he was sure that's what I had done. Run away from my problems. *Lies all lies.*

Everyone he speaks to hears his version of me. Those who know me best know cities are not for me, I hate the noise, the synthetic smell and how your neck hurts searching for the sky. I worked at McKinney's racing stable as an apprentice jockey. That is my dream and I hope... hoped someday to bring home the cups. It's not well-paid, something that irked my mum but I was dedicated. I wanted him to keep talking, that was how they would know something was wrong, something more than a missing person.

I attended Andrew's many interviews. The details never varied. On *Day 23* Andrew left the station after another fact checking interview. The latest forensic scrutiny had uncovered nothing significant. Forensics had been the team's only hope, now they had released him, possibly for the last time. I stayed behind with the officers in the small observation room. Their silence was breached by the thwack of heavy palms slamming onto the desk

'Smug bastard... he is laughing at us all... he knows there isn't one solid piece of evidence against him. He … that excuse for a man...is walking away from murder...'

Pointing at the empty chair in the interview room the detective's frustration turned to defeat and he slumped down into his chair. The inspector, a stern-faced man with broad rounding shoulders cleared his throat. A sign to his team he expected them to listen.

'I know Bria's family need something more than this... they need the truth. But knowing and proving are worlds apart. I'll speak to them, give the update. But tomorrow morning we start to review everything and reinterview all

Bria's friends especially from that group. Someone knows something.' I usually felt a warm confidence when he said my name. I was never the victim. Though I thought while the mouse changes Andrew is always the cat.

***

The lights of an approaching car don't distract Colin, he just runs on. I shout out, he doesn't hear me. The car slows to a stop, blocking his path. I see now, it's a police car. He shields his eyes, leaning forward to steady his breath. He told me once that helps with recovery, it open the lungs after exertion. Four weeks ago, he leant over just like that and emptied his dinner in the ditch, right over there. Since then, I regularly invaded his sleep trying to nudge him away from Andrew, encouraging him to do the right thing, tell the police everything. At his last interview he could hardly speak, I prayed he would tell the truth. He just clammed up and muttered Andrew's words like a dying parrot.

An officer gets out, in one fluid movement he puts on his cap and measures the situation.

'It's a bit late to be out training there now Colin.'

The officer moves closer to see his face.

'Couldn't sleep, so come out for a run' He stands straight now shrugging his shoulders, his breath still ragged.

'That right now? What's in the bag there? '

'Nothing now, its empty.'

He is moving from leg to leg like a dancing crab nodding his head at the same time, his halo of sweat caught in the law's low beam.

'Now, what does that mean? What was in it Colin? What've you been up to?'

I know what he's been up to, what he has had in his bag, but no one ever asks me. I scream, *Ask him again, what has he done? Keep asking him.*

'Get into the car here, like a good lad and we'll have a chat at the station. Let's get you settled down. What has spooked you? Have you taken something?'

'Not taken any tablets, don't do that anymore. I just run.'

Colin throws himself into the car, he seems almost relieved, no second invitation required. The door closes tight against the cold night air. Against me. Causing him unease, whispering truths each night while he sleeps seems a small torture compared to what happened to me.

It's not possible for me to go in the car or eavesdrop at the station. Each day I'm less able to move from this road. This is *Day 28,* I visited Mum and Casey. Now I've grown weak. My connection with those I love is fading as I am reeled tighter to this spot. I just know I'm nearly out of time. And I am scared.

Again, I wait and hope. Hope he breaks his silence, hope the police don't just feed him tea and biscuits and a night cell, hope the guilt flows from him like cheap wine.

He knows everything Andrew did. How my life ended. How Andrew made him carry me in his backpack and bury me here. It's always 'Andrew's Way'.

It's getting light now, must be around six in the morning. The car is back and two vans with flashing blue lights. Colin steps out of the car, hands cuffed behind his back, his head bowed. He is leading them toward me.

Leading them to my unholy grave.
The radio in the police car bursts into life. 'Sergeant, we have Andrew Jones in custody now...'

Finally, I'm found. Finally, I will have peace. That is all I wanted, for me, for my family. I'm assured there is no peace for Andrew, somehow that isn't important to me now. As my last act of substance I lean into Colin.

'Thank you... Colin. Thank you... I'll leave you now in peace.'

About the Author

Geraldine Fleming was born and raised in Northern Ireland. She retired early from an all- consuming career in social work due to ill health. Feeling bereft of purpose in life she found herself drawn into the world of creative writing. She is a member of the local North Coast Writers Group. Her poetry and prose appear in a number of anthologies and journals. Most recently, in 2022, two poems were published in Community Arts Partnership Anthology, Threshold and her poem cartographer was long listed for the Seamus Heaney Award. Short stories appeared in two new anthologies, The Heart of the Matter, Impspired Press and New Worlds New Voices, Ulster University Press.
This is her first collection of short stories. They represent her development as a writer, tapping into her creativity, drawing on experience and honing her voice. The stories are a mix of genres, what they all have in common is a deep curiosity about the human condition and how we react in different, often other worldly, situations.

Printed in Great Britain
by Amazon